WITHDRAWN

RIPE FOR REVENGE

D0965670

Also by Janie Bolitho

Kindness can kill (1993)

RIPE FOR REVENGE

Janie Bolitho

St. Martin's Press
New York

HELEN M. PLUM MEMORIAL LIBRARY
LOMBARD, ILLINOIS

RIPE FOR REVENGE. Copyright © 1994 by Janie Bolitho. All rights reserved. Printed in the United States of America. No part of this book may be used or reproduced in any manner whatsoever without written permission except in the case of brief quotations embodied in critical articles or reviews. For information, address St. Martin's Press, 175 Fifth Avenue, New York, N.Y. 10010.

Library of Congress Cataloging-in-Publication Data

Bolitho, Janie.
Ripe for revenge : a Detective Chief Inspector Roper mystery / Janie Bolitho.
191 p.   cm.
ISBN 0-312-11881-3
I. Title.
PR6052.O386R5   1995
823'.914—dc20   94-37176   CIP

First published in Great Britain by Constable & Company Ltd.

First U.S. Edition: February 1995
10 9 8 7 6 5 4 3 2 1

M
BOL

3 1502 00338 7444

For Dad,
who did not go gentle
into that good night.

1

'It's not starting again, is it, Jacko?' Janet Penhaligon asked. She waited, observing her husband as he chewed and swallowed the last mouthful of his meal. She could tell by his eyes when he was lying.

'No,' he said at last. 'I swore to you last time. I've kept my word.'

Janet's sigh of relief was drowned by the clatter of crockery as she cleared away the supper things. The thudding of her heart against her ribcage slowed a little. She stacked the plates in a bowl, squeezed a few drops of detergent over them and ran the hot tap. Last time was, and had to be, the end of it; she couldn't take any more. She had said she would leave him if it happened again and the threat still stood. Yet there had been nothing in particular about his behaviour that day that prompted her question. She was not sure why she asked. Despite his peculiarity – she could not bring herself to think of it as a perversion – she loved him.

Jacko handed her his empty tea mug, pulled on the cap which he wore all year round, and picked up the long-barrelled gun resting on its butt beside the back door.

'I'm away now. I won't be long.'

He hesitated, saw the grim pull of his wife's mouth and went off to patrol the woods without kissing her. He walked swiftly and silently, a small man, thin but wiry. His hair was almost black and his brown eyes shone out from a weather-beaten face. His colouring and features bore evidence of his Cornish ancestry. He was the first of a long line to move away from his roots – but Jacko had had a reason to.

The woods were his territory, the one area of his life where he was master. His job as protector of the trees and the wildlife that lived amongst them provided him with a sense of pride as well as a salary and the cottage which was home for himself and his family. He liked to think of himself as a gamekeeper, but really he was no more than an odd job man. The pheasants were plentiful this year but Gerald Langdon, his employer, cared little if one or two locals helped themselves to a brace. Jacko cared, and those locals knew he did, but there was no one in the woods that night.

It was only a little after ten when Janet went upstairs to check on the boys before getting ready for bed herself. She was extremely tired. Her younger child, Brian, lay flushed and tousled, one arm flung over his head, sleeping the deep sleep of a healthy eight-year-old. She kissed his forehead and pulled up the sheet, an unnecessary precaution as the night was hot and sultry. It was the instinctive act of a loving mother. She opened Michael's door. Each night she experienced the same tightness in her throat, the same despair. 'Why him, God? What has he ever done to deserve it?' she asked, knowing there was no answer.

Michael, at seventeen, was tall and well built. His movements were slow and careful and he treated anything smaller than himself with gentleness. His problem was that he had reached his intellectual capacity seven or eight years ago. The doctors were unable to give an explanation or to offer a cure. He had attended a special school until he was sixteen, and was now about to begin his second and final year at a training college in Rickenham Green. Janet knew his future was bleak. If he was lucky he might secure an undemanding job in a factory, or running errands. He had been blessed with no particular talents but he was loving and loved and sometimes spoiled by people in the village. Even his father's habits did not detract from his popularity.

After Janet learned of her son's condition it was a further nine

8

years before she was persuaded to have another child. Her GP said the chance of the same thing happening twice was remote, and time was pressing on. She was eternally grateful that she had listened.

She kissed Michael, too, then went to the bathroom to wash. It was tiny but sufficed, and they were lucky to have it at all. The previous occupant had been a solitary, crusty old man, used to roughing it and preferring to leave things as they were. When Jacko travelled up from Cornwall for an interview he explained that he had a wife and a small baby. Gerald Langdon generously said he would see that part of the largest bedroom was partitioned off and converted into a bathroom. Even at that first meeting Gerald felt there was something tragic about Jacko, that he was one of life's losers, and he wanted to give him a break. He offered him the job, knowing Jacko's history. There was no ulterior motive. His own life had been carefree and easy and his marriage was a happy one; he simply wished to repay some of this happiness. Throughout all his troubles, Gerald stood by him.

Janet brushed her teeth, her earlier suspicions forgotten, and was thankful they had come to the place, thankful for men like Gerald Langdon and that the last sixteen years had, in retrospect, held more peace than misery. But it was a difficult time for Jacko, with that Vickers child hanging round all the while. She would be glad when the kids went back to school. So far he had resisted the temptation. She hoped it would remain that way.

Ian Roper was enjoying an illicit feast. His wife, Moira, was away. Every summer she took their son, Mark, to his grandmother's for a week. On one or two occasions Ian had accompanied them but it was not his idea of a holiday. He suspected that Mark, who had just had his fifteenth birthday, also felt that way. This year, though, one of his friends had gone – Moira realized he was too old to enjoy the company of two women.

During the two weeks prior to their departure Ian had stuck

rigidly, but sulkily, to the diet she worked out for him and had lost that last, stubborn half-stone. The never-ending battle against a tightening waistband was temporarily won but he suspected the scales might tell a different story upon her return. The worst part was giving up those beloved pints of Adnams; if he had his way he would never so much as sip at a white wine and soda as long as he lived, especially the stuff – pulled from a miniature hand pump – which the landlord in The Feathers dared to call wine. It took the enamel off your teeth.

He had left work at a reasonable hour that evening. They had cleared up the building society robbery and the attempted break-in at a sub-post office. The incompetent young thieves in question were in custody, having held up their hands to both jobs and one other. The rape case which was causing some difficulty had unaccountably been dropped by the lady in question. It had never been a strong case anyway; Ian suspected she was trying to punish the man for some other reason. He enjoyed three pints of 'nectar' on his way home and began to feel light-headed. Three pints used to be no more than an aperitif; abstention was obviously not good for him. He called into the Chinese take-away and ordered a meal: sizzling beef in black bean sauce, a portion of rice, a pancake roll, and, as a sop to his conscience, some stir-fried vegetables. There were several people in the queue ahead of him so, while his order was being made up, he nipped across the road to The Crown. The landlord there, who had not seen Ian for a while, was more than surprised when he only had a half.

He collected the brown paper carrier and walked the last leg of his journey home, thinking how daft it was that over the past couple of weeks, when he hadn't been drinking, he had walked to work and back, Moira insisting he needed the exercise. Just as well he did not have the car tonight. He sat at the kitchen table, his meal spread out in front of him in its original containers because there was no sense in creating unnecessary washing-up. In one hand he held a fork, in the other a glass of decent wine. Folded so he could read it, the *Daily Mail* was propped against the wine bottle, still in its pristine condition –

10

a rare treat, as Moira managed to make it look as if she'd wrapped china in it then tried to put it back together. Ian struggled with his food for quite a while, surprised to see there was almost as much left as he'd eaten. He had become accustomed to smaller portions. Perhaps he could finish it tomorrow – except that Moira had prepared delicious, but unfilling, meals and left them in the freezer ready for him to heat up. She would know what he'd been up to if too many were left over. Besides, he wasn't sure if it was safe to reheat a Chinese, that was not his department.

Detective Chief Inspector Roper then did something of which he was vaguely ashamed. He bundled up the left-over cartons of food in several sheets of newspaper, walked to the end of Belmont Terrace and dumped the lot in a local authority waste bin, knowing his own dustbin was not due to be emptied until after Moira's return. This way saved him a justified nagging.

He belched contentedly and opened his front door in time to answer the ringing telephone. Guiltily he said, yes, he had eaten and it was delicious. Changing the subject he asked after Mark and his mother-in-law, told Moira he missed her, which was true, then settled down to watch an hour or so of television. It was Thursday. Only another three days and she'd be home, and sanity would be restored.

The village of Little Endesley lay three and a half miles west of Rickenham Green. It was one of the few outlying villages not yet swallowed up by the rapidly expanding sprawl of the town. The roads leading to it were narrow, with one or two stretches so restricted that passing places had been worn away in the grass verge by waiting cars. The branches of trees met and intertwined overhead, and in the spring, when the leaves were beginning to unfurl, driving towards Little Endesley was like entering a pale green, dappled underworld. Coming from the Rickenham direction, the road widened and opened into the village square, in the centre of which stood a war memorial dedicated to the five village men who had lost their lives

11

fighting. Around the square were one or two shops, handy for people who ran out of something, but most of their purchases were made in the supermarkets of Rickenham. The main road carried on through the village and was lined with houses and cottages. Off to one side was a small, modern development of bungalows, and forming a right angle with them was a narrow lane that rarely saw sunlight. The two-up, two-down stone cottages squeezed into it housed council tenants.

A little further up, to the right of the main street, was Vicarage Road, although the church itself was half a mile away. The building on the corner was The Pheasant, one of two pubs, neither of which was picturesque enough to draw people out from the town. There was also a greengrocer's, a butcher's, an empty building and the post office, which also served as a newsagent, off-licence and general store with a very limited stock, mostly tinned food and soap powders. The remaining buildings were more stone cottages. The Vickers family lived in the last but one.

At the end was the Vicarage, but any dubious quaintness it may have possessed was marred by the presence of a small garage whose two petrol pumps stood on the roadside and whose forecourt was invariably littered with cars in differing stages of repair. This was Little Endesley itself, but the postal address covered many other dwellings and farmhouses scattered around the neighbourhood.

Beyond the Vicarage, about a quarter of a mile up the road and a similar distance up a winding drive, stood Endesley Hall, the home of the Langdon family. In its grounds was the cottage where Janet and Jacko Penhaligon went about their precarious existence.

As far as anywhere today can be called safe, Little Endesley was such a place. There was little through traffic and it saw few strangers. Those who did arrive were soon noticed and carefully observed until the village came to some unspoken agreement as to whether they could be trusted or otherwise. The quirks of each resident were known and if a child showed signs of anxiety of fear, people knew where to look first. Jacko was the man.

The nature of a small community being what it is, Jacko was accepted, on the basis of better the devil you know. He was recognized as a hardworking man and good to his family, but no female child between the ages of six and ten was allowed near him. Michael, too, was a part of their world. His limitations were obvious but were not held against him. He had come there as a baby; people had watched him grow up and were fond of him.

It was here, in Little Endesley, during the second week of the school summer holidays, that the body of Sharon Vickers was found.

She was eight years old.

2

'Right,' Detective Chief Inspector Roper said, 'let's get it set up.'

The local sergeant at Little Endesley had received a garbled telephone call from Jim Black. It took him several minutes to decipher what Black was talking about. Mrs Black had come running into the house in a terrible state. She'd been walking the dog. Jim had had to shake her several times before she was able to tell him she'd found the body of a child. She'd felt for a pulse, although she was not absolutely certain how this was done, but knew already it was useless. Jim Black, when he himself was coherent, passed this information on to the appropriate person, in the form of Sergeant Bob Davies. He, in turn, immediately rang the area headquarters in Rickenham.

'Haven't seen it for myself yet, sir,' he told the Chief, to whom he had been put through. 'Thought I ought to let you know at once. But I know the Blacks, pleasant, retired couple, the wife's not the hysterical sort, not one to make such a thing up. I'm on my way up there now.'

Sergeant Davies was instructed to get Mrs Black to show him exactly where the body lay and they were to remain there until reinforcements arrived. Hopefully no one else had come across it or disturbed it in any way. 'She can wait in the car – Mrs Black. Park it so she doesn't have to look at the child. You can get a car up there? Good. The troops'll be with you almost at once. You can give them the exact location from the car.' The troops, Bob Davies knew, consisted of a photographer, scene-

14

of-crime officers, plan-makers, forensics and anyone else he cared to name who make up a murder squad.

Sergeant Davies followed his instructions to the letter, just as he always did and always would. He radioed through the quickest route as soon as he was able.

Sharon Vickers' lifeless body lay a few yards off a track leading through the woods, a track wide enough to take a vehicle, even one as wide as a Land Rover, which Jacko Penhaligon sometimes drove. His was the first name to be mentioned.

'It's been over three years now, sir,' Bob reminded the chief when he arrived at the scene. 'And he's never been violent.' Bob prided himself that he knew, if not every individual in the village, then at least one member of each family. He had been posted to Little Endesley fourteen years previously and was a most unusual man in that he was perfectly content with his lot. He did not want to move, he did not desire promotion. And he was glad the old days were gone when you were moved from pillar to post at the drop of a hat. Neither did he understand the sniggers and sighs of relief when he was appointed to that outlying area. The young ones wanted to make a name for themselves amongst the concrete and glass of the town, he supposed, but what better way to do it than to be known and respected by a whole community? And his wife, Dorothy – who could ask for a better companion? Not only did she keep perfect house for him but answered any calls when he was out on his rounds fighting crime as he laughingly called it. Ironic really: when there was a spate of poaching, or travellers, as the gypsies were now called, camping illegally in the woods, he worked alongside Jacko. At other times he was bringing him in for questioning before the Rickenham lot took over. Bob Davies was aware of his good fortune. Most villages no longer had their own police house and local bobby. When he retired in eighteen months' time, nor would Little Endesley. Someone from Rickenham would patrol the area.

Well, someone from Rickenham would certainly want a word with Jacko now.

15

The red ball of the sun was barely visible through the thick, dusty foliage of the trees as it sank in the sky. Elsewhere it was dusk, but in the woods it was dark when Sharon's body was removed. Harsh arc lamps lit the grisly scene and every man present felt that nothing, not even the bloodiest killing, was worse than having to answer a call involving the death of a young child, and not one of them wanted to be given the task of informing her parents.

Ian Roper, as senior man, could delegate this to anyone, but felt it was a moral cop-out. He should do it himself, along with a WPC. His relief was heartfelt when Sergeant Davies volunteered to go and see them, along with Dorothy, if that didn't go against police protocol. Whether it did or not, Ian felt it was the most humane way, the news coming from two people they knew and trusted. He gave his permission.

'Stay with the Vickers as long as you like. We'll be packing up here in a minute, it's up to the experts for now.'

Mrs Black gave an initial statement while she sat in the car trying not to turn round to see what was happening behind her. She didn't really want to know, but the force of ghoulish curiosity was strong. Sergeant Davies dropped her off at her home and left her in the hands of her husband with directions to make some hot, strong tea and to put a drop of something in it. Then he went on to collect his own wife.

It was after this that Detective Chief Inspector Roper said, 'Right, let's get it set up.' He was referring to the mobile incident centre. Rickenham was, for the moment, too far away to operate from and the police house where Bob Davies lived was not suitable – he had to use his own front room for interviews. This way, a police presence was far more visible, a constant reminder to people whose memories might need jogging.

Although it was Mrs Black who found the body, it was Bob Davies who identified it. He was shocked, as much as Mrs Black had been, but managed not to show it. The child had not been reported missing, no child had for a long time, and the last one had turned up, unharmed, with what was, to the child, a perfectly valid excuse for its absence. Any call concerning a child was taken seriously – with Jacko on the doorstep it had to be. A murder was not a possibility Bob Davies had contemplated: it was the first in his time in the village. For once he felt nothing but respect for the 'city boys' who dealt with such matters daily.

The incident centre was put into place in the village square with much noise and disturbance. Technicians worked quickly to ensure telephones and other necessary equipment worked efficiently. Occasionally, under such circumstances, the local village or church hall was requisitioned but Little Endesley possessed a tiny one and that was stacked with boxes of jumble, paperback books and pots of home-made everything in readiness for the summer fête.

Ian picked up the telephone and dialled his home number, only remembering on the third ring that Moira was away. Old habits die hard. She never nagged or complained, whatever the hour of night he returned, but she preferred it if he rang to say he'd be late so she need not wait up.

Sergeant Davies sent a message to say that Mr and Mrs Vickers had been told the news and that it was Mr Vickers who was to make the official identification. He had had a difficult time persuading his wife it was for the best. Sharon was in no way mutilated. The police surgeon would close her eyes and shut away the startled look which remained in them. That, perhaps, was the only consolation.

Mrs Black had come across the body at approximately five o'clock. It was the dog who drew her attention to it although no attempt had been made to hide it. The undergrowth was thick enough to conceal such a small bundle temporarily. Doc Harris, the divisional police surgeon, estimated the time of death as about two hours before his examination, about four p.m. The cause of death was asphyxiation, but they would need to wait for the post-mortem results to be sure there were no other internal injuries. So, Ian decided, all they needed to ascertain was where everyone was between, say, two and five that afternoon. It sounded very simple. Finding the murderer would not restore the child to life but the parents might gain some comfort once the killer was locked away. And not just the Vickers, but all the other parents who, once they heard, would be terrified to let their children out of sight. These things were so much easier to deal with in term-time. One of his men would go along to the school and talk to each class in turn, warning them strongly of the danger and impressing upon them the importance of letting someone know exactly where they were at all times. Notes could be sent to the parents requesting them to escort their children to school and to collect them afterwards, their safety being more or less guaranteed whilst they were there. But in the holidays? How was it possible to keep kids at home in this weather?

Supposing this was no local, no one from Rickenham where they might have a chance of catching him, but someone who was passing through – an opportunist stranger who simply happened to come across Sharon – what then? Would he ever be found, or was Little Endesley to be plagued by fear and suspicion for a very long time?

There was no point in suppositions. How often did he reprimand his men for acting on suppositions or assumptions? Facts were required, facts and the inevitable paperwork. Computers and cross-referencing, statements and interviews, all checked and rechecked until a discrepancy came to light, until a lie was discovered. Firstly, house-to-house inquiries before people started going to bed.

And he must interview Mr and Mrs Vickers. Tonight. He didn't want to do it.

He briefed the officers who had been made available, stressing that he wanted every man, woman and child in the village questioned. Tonight preferably, but if that was not possible, tomorrow morning, without fail. Using a large-scale map of the area, which was spread out on the incident room table and held down at the corners with an assortment of objects, he delegated the areas they were to cover. Then he told a WPC who had arrived with the initial party to accompany him. He walked with her towards the Vickers' house, aware of, but ignoring,

18

the twitching net curtains. Ian did not think the news would have circulated yet, not unless Mrs Black and her husband were inveterate gossips. They did not give that impression and Mrs Black was still in shock and not likely to want to talk to anyone but her husband about it yet. The inhabitants, however, could scarcely have failed to notice the eyesore of the mobile unit, set smack in the middle of the square.

'Done this sort of thing before?' Ian asked, more by way of breaking the silence than out of real interest. The WPC at his side was young and not particularly attractive. A bad case of teenage acne had left her face pockmarked, and her hair, or what was visible under her uniform cap, looked dull and lank.

'Yes, sir. Once.' WPC Livingstone, new to Rickenham Green, was respectful and stolid and unafraid of hard work. Unlike some women officers, she did not suffer at the hands of her male colleagues. She was too plain and lacked the personality to make up for her looks to attract their attention.

'Oh? Not since you've been with us?'

'No, sir. Ipswich. Two years ago.' Her manner of speech was abrupt, businesslike. Ian took a surreptitious sideways glance. Two years ago? She hardly seemed old enough to have completed her training. Of course, the old adage about policemen appearing younger also applied to females. He nearly said as much but was taken aback by her adult, no-nonsense attitude. Momentarily he forgot the gravity of the situation. 'No,' he thought, 'it isn't that I've forgotten, it's because I'm trying to get the picture of little Sharon Vickers out of my mind.' He did not want to think about it. If he, an outsider, and supposedly a professional one, felt this way, how much worse it must be for her parents.

'Two years ago? Not the Robertson case, surely?' His interest was genuine now.

'Yes, sir. The Robertson case.'

Ian left it at that. Patricia Livingstone, never the most forthcoming of individuals, kept her eyes to the front. That topic of conversation was clearly at an end. Ian took the hint, the girl did not need any reminders of that atrocity. Two children,

19

brother and sister, had been brutally murdered in their own home whilst their mother was next door chatting to a neighbour. It was one of those senseless things. How could their mother have realized that in the supposed safety of their own back garden her children could be wiped out in the space of ten minutes? The Ipswich police had not had to look far. Like most murders, it was committed by someone known to the family, in this case the husband's unstable stepbrother.

They arrived at the Vickers' house and knocked at the door. Pat Livingstone barely reached the shoulder of her superior officer. Ian stood at six feet four inches and there were many occasions when he found his size useful. He was a gentle man but in a tight corner, people would think twice before upsetting him. WPC Livingstone saw him rub the palms of his hands together but did not know him well enough to realize this was a characteristic gesture, a thing he did to prepare himself for unpleasantness.

Dorothy Davies opened the door to them. 'Bob's still here,' she whispered. 'It hasn't sunk in with them yet. Don't suppose it will until tomorrow,' she added knowledgeably, having assisted her husband in other, less violent bereavements. 'I'll make some more tea.' She opened the door of the front room.

DCI Roper and his companion made their visit as brief as possible. Tonight they merely wanted to find out where, when and by whom Sharon was last seen. Tomorrow they would be questioned more thoroughly but there was a limit to what people could take. Ian, hating himself, used the clichéd phrases to express his sorrow but, as always, was glad of them. Left to find words for himself what could he have possibly said?

Julie Vickers, her pretty face altered out of recognition by grief, blamed herself. 'I shouldn't have let her out,' she kept insisting. 'I should've made sure she stayed with the boys.' Dorothy Davies put her plump, motherly arm around her and held her while she rocked backwards and forwards in her chair.

Tom Vickers sat with his head in his hands, tears streaming down his face. 'I can't believe it, I just can't believe it. Not

Sharon. Please tell me it's a mistake,' he said, looking at Ian, a mixture of misery and hope in his eyes.

'I'm sorry, Mr Vickers, it's not a mistake. But we'll get whoever's responsible, you can be sure of that.' How Ian hoped he was right. 'It might seem callous, but are you up to answering a few questions.'

'If it'll help catch the bastard I'll do anything.'

What Tom Vickers had to tell them was of little use except in providing himself with an alibi. Ian did not believe he had killed his own daughter but the man's statement would have to be substantiated. He hoped he would not discover that his movements had been investigated.

Astutely, Ian assessed the couple in front of him. As was often the case, the wife, for the moment, appeared the stronger of the two. Later, when she had seen the rest of the family through it, she would have her turn to mourn.

'Mrs Vickers? Where's your son now?'

'Ronnie's next door. I couldn't bear him to see us like this.'

'Mrs Vickers, please don't be offended at my suggestion, but mightn't he feel pushed out if he can't share your sorrow? Mightn't he think he's in some way to blame and you don't want him here?'

'Oh, God, no. I didn't mean it like that. Oh poor Ronnie.' She stood up, swaying slightly. 'I'll get him right away.'

'You sit there, love. I'll fetch him,' Dorothy said. The tea which he had brought in on a carefully laid tray remained untouched.

'Do you want to ask him questions?' Julie Vickers said.

Ian nodded. 'Only one or two for the time being. We'll leave most of them until tomorrow.'

Ronnie appeared, holding tightly to Dorothy's hand. His face was deathly pale and he was trembling. He did not look as if he'd been crying.

'Hello, Ronnie. I'm Detective Chief Inspector Roper, and this is WPC Livingstone. I expect you know why we're here.'

Ronnie looked down at his feet.

Ian dropped down on to one knee. Ronnie was ten, but small for his age, and Ian knew how large and frightening he would appear, especially under the circumstances. 'Can you tell me, Ronnie, when did you last see Sharon?'

And then the tears started. Ian didn't think he'd ever witnessed such an enormous amount of pain in such a small body. He rested a hand on his shoulder; he was uncomfortable, aware that he did not know the best way to deal with the child. His mother came to the rescue. 'It's all right, love, just tell the man what he wants to know. No one's blaming you, it's not your fault.'

Incoherently Ronnie blurted out that Sharon had gone with him and his friends then changed her mind. 'She said she didn't want to play with us. She went off on her own.'

'Can you remember what time?'

'No, mister, but it wasn't long after we left here.'

Ian and Pat took their leave. The family was too distraught to think clearly; they would come back tomorrow. There had been one moment of danger when Tom Vickers, showing the first sign of animation since the beginning of their visit, suddenly jumped out of his seat, threatening to go up and kill Jacko Penhaligon with his bare hands. It was Sergeant Davies who calmed him down and promised to stay a bit longer.

'It still could be Jacko,' Ian said, more to himself than to his companion, as they headed back to the mobile unit. 'A girl like that – you heard what her mother said. She was different from other eight-year-olds, always hanging around with boys slightly older than herself. Often on her own, and mature for her age. Maybe she wasn't having any and put up a bit of a fight. Could've got the wind up Jacko and he silenced her.'

'No history of it though, is there, sir?' Pat said. 'I know we can't write him off but from the little I've heard of him, he's more the type to run at the first sign of trouble.'

Well, well, Ian thought sardonically. Sharon Vickers was not run of the mill, but neither was WPC Livingstone. Usually new staff, especially females, were afraid to express themselves freely in front of someone like himself, who far outranked them;

this one had no such qualms. He wondered if she was another Judy Robbins in the making. Judy was a good policewoman, reliable and steady, but she took no nonsense from anyone, especially Sergeant Swan, with whom Ian was partnered. She frequently expressed her opinion of his vanity, his treatment of women and his high self-regard. If he was being totally over-bearing she knew where to strike. His height. Barry Swan's only desire was to be several inches taller.

The night was warm and the scent of summer flowers hung in the air. A few people were still in their gardens, chatting or sipping a drink, enjoying every minute of England's unpredict-able weather. The door of the unit was open. Inside, sitting on a metal tubular chair and nervously smoking a roll-up, was Jacko Penhaligon.

'He's not saying anything, sir,' Detective Sergeant Swan informed him.

'I'm innocent,' Jacko proclaimed in the manner of many well-known criminals. It was an automatic reaction. 'I never done nothing, I don't care what anyone says.'

'And why should you think anyone has said something?' Barry Swan continued, as stubborn in his own way as the man he was interviewing. He was not averse to asking the same questions as many times as were needed until he got the right answer.

'Come on, Jacko, you know all this hasn't been set up with the sole purpose of harassing you.' The Chief indicated their surroundings with a sweeping movement of his arm. 'If you're as innocent as you say, what harm is there in answering our questions?'

'You'll pin it on me either way, that's what harm there is. Whatever I say you'll twist my words to suit yourselves.'

'OK,' Sergeant Swan continued, 'either you tell us where you were or we'll take you into Rickenham and you can spend the night courtesy of the government, and from what I remember, I don't think your wife'll take too kindly to that. I seem to recall after that last bit of trouble – '

'All right, you bastard,' Jacko shouted, half out of his chair.

23

'I'll tell you, then maybe you'll leave me alone.' Jacko took several sharp pulls on his dog end before extinguishing it in the blackened lid of an old tobacco tin. The Chief watched him, noting his anxiety but also wondering how, if pipe tobacco now came in polythene pouches, these tins or their lids could still be found in every police station in the land. They waited. 'All right,' Jacko said sullenly, 'from what time?'

'Let's start from midday.' The Chief didn't want to give him clues.

'I was up at the Hall. Mr Langdon wanted a word with me about two of them trees in the top coppice. One of 'em's dying and another's dead, and they're right alongside the public footpath. A strong wind and branches could come down, and it wouldn't do if someone was underneath, like, at the time. Might lead to a court case, and it wouldn't do for him to have anything like that, not a man in his position.' Jacko was not being cynical; he was a man who thought it was acceptable for someone like himself to appear in court, but not Mr Langdon, he was far too nice. He was his employer's biggest admirer and was fully aware of the man's loyalty to him. That loyalty worked both ways. 'Well, I said they should be cut down, he can use the timber for firewood come the winter. The sooner the better. I left about a quarter to one. You can check,' he added, brown eyes glaring from his monkey-like face.

'Oh we will, Jacko, we will.' This, from Sergeant Swan. As he said it he realized that policemen, including himself, address the criminal fraternity by their first, or even nicknames, and everyone else as Mr or Mrs, or sir or madam. Now was not the time to ponder over this minor piece of psychology.

'And after that?'

'Went home for me dinner. Wife'll tell you.' In other situations the alibi would count for little, but Janet Penhaligon was a totally honest woman. In all his past history she had never given a false alibi for her husband. If she said he came home for his dinner at that time, then he did. They would, of course, ask her. 'Then, about two I suppose it was, I walked up through the woods and across the field to have another look at the trees

24

and to mark them. Had to tie strips of orange plastic round them, I wanted to make sure those tree surgeon people don't make no mistakes.' Jacko sniffed, his contempt for such people was obvious. It was beyond him why he, who possessed a perfectly adequate chain saw, couldn't do it himself.

'And who did you see in your travels?' Sergeant Swan asked. 'I mean, a beautiful, sunny afternoon – there must have been quite a few people about?'

'No one.'

'No one? And how long were you up at the coppice?' As he asked the question, Barry made a note to send a man to walk from Jacko's cottage to where the trees stood to see just how long it took.

'Gawd, I don't know. Half an hour at the most. I marked the damn things then I sat down to have a fag. No crime in that, I suppose?' No mistaking the sarcasm this time.

'Then you returned through the woods?' Ian took over. They were playing the double act, one they were used to; sometimes it served to confuse a suspect.

Jacko's head gave an involuntary jerk. A line of sweat glistened on his upper lip. He nodded.

'You walked back through the woods. Who did you see?'

'No one. I didn't see anyone. I don't know what you're on about, why can't you leave me alone?'

'Because,' Ian said quietly, 'I think you're lying. Because I think you did see someone or something and because I think . . .' but he knew he could not continue. Alone, he might have told Jacko Penhaligon what he thought of him, and men like him, but he knew better than to do so in front of witnesses. Instead he said, 'You saw no one at all, on a day like today? Surely there were people walking dogs, kids playing, ramblers, the whole world out enjoying itself, yet you saw no one. Odd, wouldn't you say? And when you'd walked back through the woods, what did you do then?'

'Went home for my tea.' There was a finality about the remark, as if the interview must now come to an end. But he did not add, 'You can ask the wife.'

25

'You went home for your tea. Let me refresh my memory,' Ian said, scratching his head as if he genuinely needed to. 'You had your dinner and left home at about two. You spent half an hour or so doing whatever was necessary to the trees, then you went home for your tea. Long walk, is it, from your house to the coppice?'

Jacko missed the innuendo. He looked at his interrogators as if they were stupid; they knew exactly where he lived and he bet they knew where the coppice was.

'Course not, about fifteen minutes.'

'I see.' Ian paused then said, as if something was puzzling him, 'Would you say you have a large appetite?'

It was Jacko's turn to be surprised. He'd endured quite a few grillings in the hands of the Old Bill, sometimes with just cause, sometimes not, but he'd never been asked a question which seemed so irrelevant.

'What d'you mean by that?'

'A simple enough question, I'd've thought. You do manual work, you're out in the fresh air most of the time and from what I hear, you're no slacker, you must build up quite an appetite.'

'No more than the next man. I'm not exactly obese, am I?' His Cornish accent was becoming more pronounced, the vowels more drawn out. It was a sure sign he was worried.

'No more than the next man. Would you explain?'

Jacko was totally bewildered. What his eating habits had to do with anything was a mystery, but there was no harm in answering the question, especially if it diverted their attention away from the main issue. He produced from his ill-fitting trouser's pocket the makings of another roll-up.

'I have a breakfast,' he said, taking a pinch of tobacco and placing it on the paper. 'A proper one, mark you. Then a bit of dinner.' He paused to lick the paper, expertly sealing the contents and glanced at his handiwork almost with admiration. Ian knew the trick. When he'd smoked he'd used it too, sometimes a a diversionary tactic, sometimes to play for time.

'Dinner's usually soup and bread, or a couple of sandwiches, a snack really.' He struck a match and lit up. It didn't make much difference, the enclosed space was already foul from the smoke of the previous one and the air was still, no breeze came through the open door to relieve them. 'Janet cooks in the evenings so's we can all eat together, even in the holidays. If there's anything left over I have it for my supper. I look forward to that, especially if I've had to go out again – another plate of cold meat and veg goes down a treat.'

The game had gone on long enough. Ian decided to bring it to an end.

'This evening meal, you call it tea, you eat it at what time? About six?'

Jacko was watching the end of his cigarette, it was not burning evenly. 'Yes, about then.'

'So where were you? You have your meal at six, but by my calculations you returned home no later than three thirty. Bit early, wasn't it?'

The cigarette was between Jacko's middle finger and thumb. He held it over the makeshift ashtray to knock off the ash but he shook too much to do this accurately.

Now he understood the line of their questioning. How foolish he'd been. Of course it was too early. But he'd panicked. Whatever he said now they were not going to believe and it was his own fault. He should have told the truth to begin with.

'Well, Jacko?'

'I was in the wood, that's where I was. Then I took a walk. I just walked.' It was hopeless, they knew men like him didn't just take a walk, there was always some purpose to it. But not that afternoon. He had needed to walk to think what to do.

'Why didn't you say so before?'

'I don't bloody know.' He was angry with himself and it made him belligerent. He'd been tricked. He should have come out with it before. Still, it would only have led to the same thing. 'I don't know.' He banged a calloused fist on the table. 'All I know is that whatever I say you'll try to pin it on me.'

'Pin what on you?'

Oh no, not this time, he didn't fall a second time. 'Whatever it is you're investigating. How the hell should I know?'

Ian shrugged. There was not enough evidence to hold him, none really, only his admission that he was in the area at around the right time, but so were other people.

'OK, Jacko, that's all for tonight. You know the form, stay where we can find you.'

He didn't deign to answer and left without saying another word.

'What do you think?

Barry sighed. 'Difficult to say. He's lying, there's no doubt about that, but it's second nature to him where we're concerned. But he also knows we wouldn't have picked him up unless it was something to do with a child. Do we know if he's got any other form?'

'Not as far as I know. Better double check. Get back to Rickenham and pull his files, and while you're at it find out who's head man with the Devon and Cornwall lot and have a word. Could be something we've missed.'

Meanwhile, throughout the village, people were being dragged away from their television sets and their videos. Because it was Friday, not everyone was at home. Quite a few were in one or other of the two pubs, some had gone into Rickenham in search of livelier entertainment and would not return home until very late, too late to be seen that night. Two or three families were away on holiday. The Chief wanted an account of everyone's movements and he wanted it within twenty-four hours; but more importantly he wanted to know what they'd seen or heard that was in any way suspicious or different from the norm.

The officers knocking on doors were used to the variety of responses they received. They ranged from unashamed curiosity to a willingness to help so great that facts were invented. Occasionally a caring member of the general public wished to drop someone in it. Some were furtive, evasive, wondering if a small dismeanour had come to light. The most common reaction that evening, because the start of the weekend was being ruined, was sullen non-cooperation.

Doc Harris promised to do the post-mortem first thing in the morning, forgoing his Saturday round of golf with Superintendent Ross, which was a dubious pleasure at the best of times. He only played as a vague attempt to keep fit and counteract the forty or so cigarettes he got through each day, a vice he shared with the head of SOC, John Cotton.

Once Sergeant Swan had set off for Rickenham, the Chief headed in the opposite direction. He was going to Endesley Hall to interview Mr Langdon. The reason for his visit was twofold. Firstly the crime was committed on his property, and, secondly, he knew him.

Gerald Langdon and his wife were holding a dinner party. Nothing grand, just themselves and two other couples. The village looked upon the Langdons as if they were landed gentry but they were not really wealthy, only by comparison. They employed three people: Jacko, whose responsibilities were the woods, keeping the public foothpath clear, and all the odd jobs inside and outside the house; a lady named Mrs Dennis who came in twice a week to help with the housework and do the occasional bit of ironing; and Eileen Butterfield who helped with the potting, thinning and delivery of the bedding plants and hardy annuals Sonia Langdon grew to supplement their income. Sonia did all the cooking herself. Not only did she enjoy it, anything she produced was always delicious.

Gerald, outside the small living he made from leasing out most of his land, made his money as a solicitor in Ipswich. Since the day he inherited Endesley Hall he had thanked his father for insisting on a good education. If he were not a partner in the firm for which he worked, the family home would have had to be sold. The land was no longer a viable proposition. His own boys were being brought up in the same vein. They went to the village school, which David, the younger, still attended. Peter, who was eleven, was to go to Hazeldown School in

Rickenham at the beginning of next term. In Gerald's day it had been the local grammar school. Peter, like the rest of the village children, was to make the journey by the school bus.

The Chief drove carefully up the gravel drive, not wishing to mar the paintwork on his ancient Rover, his pride and joy. He parked alongside a couple of cars and realized the Langdons had company. It was Gerald himself who opened the door, looking extremely surprised to see him standing there.

'Ian! What brings you to this neck of the woods? Nothing serious, I hope?'

'I'd like a word or two if you can spare a few minutes.'

Gerald knew by his tone it was serious. 'Of course. Sonia and I have some friends here, bit of a dinner. I'll just make my excuses.' Before doing so he showed Ian into a large room to the left of the passage. There were windows on both sides, overlooking both the front drive and the lawn and a path which ran round the side of the house, beyond which were two fairly big greenhouses. Once the room had been a library. There were still many books lining the shelves set against one of the windowless walls but the desk was a mess, covered in folders and files and pieces of paper. From where he stood, Ian saw that some of it was connected with the estate but many of the files were an overflow from Langdon's office in Ipswich. In a corner was a small table holding a sewing machine; beneath it the carpet was strewn with pieces of loose cotton. Sonia was in the process of making a dress. In the few seconds before he sat down, Ian took all this in. Rooms and their contents held many clues to the personalities of the occupants. There was nothing sinister here.

Gerald returned, bearing a tray with two glasses and a decanter.

'Brandy, Ian? Might help oil the wheels. I'd drink it instead of wine with my food, but there we are, not the done thing.'

Ian was technically on duty but he had come alone and was therefore not going to be taking a formal statement. He would bend the rules. One drink could do no harm; it might help to quell the nausea he felt each time he thought of Sharon Vickers' lifeless body.

'Thanks, Gerald, but make it a small one.'

'Here. Cheers. Now what's happened?' Several things ran through Gerald's mind – gypsies, poachers, stolen livestock and Jacko – but nothing that approached the real reason for Ian's visit.

'I'm sorry, Gerald, but the body of a child was found on your land this afternoon. Sharon Vickers. Eight years old.'

'Oh no. Not Sharon. God, how awful.'

'You knew her?'

'Yes, of course. Well, in a way. She's the same age as David, they're, they were, in the same class, and she was often about the place.'

'She came up here?'

'Occasionally. She would watch Sonia with her planting, taking it all in with big eyes, Sonia said – didn't say much, though. Sometimes I saw her roaming around the woods. She struck me as . . . I'm not sure what – different somehow. Perhaps it was the way she looked at you, as if she was the elder. She's been coming up here ever since she was about five. At first she used to try to play with David and Peter, but you know what boys are like – they were cruel in a way, they told her to push off, they didn't want to play with girls. But I can't believe she, of all kids, would go off with a stranger. I take it that's what's happened?'

'We don't know yet. You didn't mind her being on your property?'

Gerald seemed surprised by the question. 'No, why should I? Besides, only part of the woods are private, don't forget there's the public footpath through the bit to the south. And as for the rest of the land, as long as the kids keep off the crops, they're welcome to play there.'

'And Jacko Penhaligon?'

'Ah, yes.' Gerald sat down, watching his brandy, as he swirled it in the glass. 'I rather thought his name would crop

31

up sooner or later. Poor bugger. It's an awful thing to admit, but as soon as I saw you I wondered if he'd been at it again. But it's been ages, hasn't it, since the last time?'

'Yes, a couple of years or more, and I know this isn't his style. Exposing yourself to small children is one thing, killing them is another matter. But we have to be certain.'

'You've spoken to him already?' It must be awful to have the police on your doorstep every time something happened.

'We have, but unfortunately we know part of what he told us isn't true.'

'Before you continue, I can tell you where he was for at least part of the day. He spent the morning mostly here. There were a couple of loose panes in the greenhouse – he replaced them, then he tinkered around with the Land Rover. For a man that's never owned his own car he's a marvel with engines. However, most of the time I could see him from that window.' Ian saw that from the chair behind Gerald's desk the greenhouses and the double garage would clearly have been visible, as indeed they were now, with outside lights blazing. 'He had his coffee in the kitchen then came in to see me. On Fridays I usually give him a list of what I want doing the following week, and I especially wanted him to have a look at a couple of suspect trees. He left about, oh, quarter or ten to one. Certainly not before that.'

'And then?'

'He went off home for his lunch. He said he'd mark the trees this afternoon, and if he said he would, I'm sure he has.'

So far Jacko's story was one hundred per cent correct. Ian did not suspect Gerald Langdon of lying but he reminded himself that, although it was highly improbable, it was possible.

'Did you see him again after that?'

'No, I didn't, but you'd better have a word with Sonia, she may have wanted him for something.' Gerald paused. 'Look, I know a lot of people can't understand why I keep him on, but he's a hard-working man, always willing to do whatever I ask, and he works for a salary I can afford to pay. True, he also has a roof over his head but that cottage would fall into dereliction if it wasn't inhabited. Despite what he's done in the past I really can't believe he's killed a child. Sorry, Ian, had to have my say. I'll go and fetch Sonia. Will you need me again? One of us should play the host.'

'No. I don't think so. Someone'll be round tomorrow to take a formal statement from you both, and the staff. Apart from Jacko, who was here today?'

'Eileen Butterfield. In the greenhouse all day. The heat doesn't seem to bother her, must be over a hundred in there in this weather. Mrs Dennis doesn't come on Fridays.'

'Thanks, Gerald.' Ian took a deep breath. This was the hard part. 'Just before you go, I have to ask, could you give me a quick run-down on your own movements today?'

Gerald nodded. 'No need for embarrassment, I wondered when you'd get round to it. You mean why wasn't I in the office? Never am on Fridays. It's the day I do all the estate paperwork, pay the wages, etc. Monday to Thursday I work late, to make up for it, and if I'm really pushed I go in over the weekend – it's easier then, anyway, without the phones ringing. I also bring work home with me.' He indicated the untidy desk-top. 'I was here in this room all morning. Eileen Butterfield will bear that out; she must have been able to see me from where she was working. After lunch I went into Rickenham to the bank. I left there about three and popped into The Crown, it's open all day on Fridays.' Ian already knew that, and not just because he was a detective. 'I was there longer than I intended, over an hour. Got into a convoluted conversation with the landlord, he'll remember because there was hardly anyone in there. Then I came home and read through a file that's been causing some problems, which didn't leave me long to shower and change ready for our guests. Both couples arrived more or less together, about seven.'

'And you noticed nothing unusual today, no one hanging around who shouldn't have been?'

'No, sorry, I didn't. I wasn't really looking for anything, though.' He thought for a while and shook his head. 'No, absolutely nothing comes to mind.'

'Thanks again, Gerald. I apologize for having to . . .'

Gerald held up a conciliatory hand. 'No need. I understand. Part of the job. I'll go and get Sonia.'

Sonia merely corroborated what her husband had said. Ian, who had only met her once or twice, judged her to be as open and honest as the man she had married. He could not believe either of them would harm a child. He apologized a second time for interrupting their evening and made his farewells. Climbing into the comfortable security of his car he started the engine, enjoyed anew the split second when it purred into life, and drove back to the village proper, grimly reflecting that although their meal had been interrupted he had provided them with a topic of conversation which would surely see them through to the port.

He checked that the door-to-door inquiries were well under way, picked up some paperwork from the mobile unit and went back to Rickenham Green. They were as much in the dark at headquarters as in Little Endesley. He went home and, surprisingly, slept well.

3

Alan Campbell was Scottish and proud of it. He supported Partick Thistle and was overjoyed when they were promoted at the end of the 1991/92 season. Apart from Detective Chief Inspector Roper, who had his own peculiarities where football was concerned, he was unfortunate in that there was no one else to share his jubilation when 'The Jags' went up. Everyone was more concerned with the efforts of the England team. The Chief and Alan also held many conversations along those lines, each putting forward his opinion concerning the deficiencies or otherwise of his own national side. The Chief had admitted that he went to watch Norwich if he had a free Saturday and that this was a bone of contention between himself and his son who told him plainly that if he was daft enough to stand in the freezing cold for ninety minutes, he should at least support the local league team. In Ian's case this was Ipswich.

He also confessed that he had taken Mark to the final match at the end of last season because he had been accused of neglecting the boy. Only later did he remember that Mark did not share his enthusiasm and must have been totally bored by the whole thing.

Alan suffered similar trials. On one occasion, with a free weekend coming up, he saved enough to pay for two stand-by plane tickets to Glasgow and a night in a reasonable hotel and took his wife, Helen, up to watch The Thistle. The nil-nil draw did little to fire her enthusiasm, which was on a par with Mark's.

No one could mistake Alan for anything other than Scottish. Although the Glaswegian brogue of his childhood was watered down after fifteen years in the south, the accent was still unmistakable. His hair was sandy, his eyes a piercing blue and, winter or summer, his skin remained the same bluish-white, dusted with a sprinkling of gingery freckles. Five minutes of hot, August sunshine was enough to raise blisters. Across his top lip lay a thin moustache, slightly darker than his hair. It went some way towards alleviating the pinched, city-boy look with which he was afflicted. When he saw his reflection in a mirror he was amazed that someone like Helen had ever been interested in him in the first place, let alone enough to marry him. They had little in common yet their marriage worked.

Helen was the outdoor type. She loved swimming and tennis and sunbathing. Unlike her husband, her skin turned golden brown. She also enjoyed eating out but it was not a thing they often did. Conversely, Alan had a morbid dread of water, thought football was the only sport worth mentioning and couldn't understand when Helen took herself upstairs to read whenever he watched it on television. His strict, puritanical upbringing had left its mark. He believed eating in restaurants was a disgraceful waste of money, that it was almost immoral to pay for a piece of meat, smothered in a sauce, when the same meal could be plainly cooked at home for a tenth of the cost. It had taken a long time for Helen to introduce him to green vegetables and to methods of cooking other than frying. He was still fussy, but at least their food was a little more varied.

They had been married for almost nine years and despite the fact than they had stopped using any method of contraception six years ago, they still had no children. At first they had discussed the possibility of adoption, but now they were not concerned; they were happy the way they were, just the two of them. Helen continued with her job as a local government secretary. It was an interesting post and gave them another topic of conversation apart from 'the job'. And, of course, the money was useful.

Alan Campbell was thirty and not a likely candidate for

promotion. He worked conscientiously and was, quite often, over-meticulous, but he did not possess what his colleagues referred to as 'the nose': that instinct which told you when you were on the right track even when there was not a scrap of evidence to substantiate it.

He had recently transferred to CID, partly because he was tired of slogging the streets, but also because the hours would mean he saw more of Helen.

Ian Roper authorized the transfer, warning him that if he didn't come up to the mark he would be back in uniform. Alan took the warning seriously. Ian recognized Campbell's willingness to perform tasks less inviting to some of the men. Few people were capable of such consistent vigilance; boredom and slackness often set in. But these tasks were nonetheless vital. Statements had to be co-ordinated and filed, the same ground had to be covered again and again until a discrepancy was found. It took a lot of doggedness to retain that initial energy. Alan never gave up. If there was a connection, however tenuous, between any of the facts in his possession, Alan would find it.

On Friday evening, when Detective Constable Campbell learned of Sharon Vickers' murder, he knew his services would be required over the weekend. He might not be out on the streets, he would not be the one hauling people in for questioning, but he would wholeheartedly be doing his bit.

He was clearing up a few bits and pieces on his desk when Barry Swan rang him and asked him to come in on Saturday morning and, he added, 'to hell with the overtime restrictions.' Alan knew Helen would be disappointed because they had tentatively made plans to go out for the day. He liked Sergeant Swan and wished he was more like him. The man was handsome and quick-thinking and exuded confidence. Alan was not aware that Barry treated him kindly and with tolerance because he loathed paperwork, and worse, because he regarded him as no threat to his own career.

When Alan arrived home Helen was watching television. 'As soon as this is finished I'll get the meal,' she said as he kissed

37

the top of her head. He sat down, glad of a few minutes in which to mentally switch off. He watched his wife as she took another sip of the drink she'd already poured and lit a cigarette. The Highland puritanism rose to the surface. Whenever he saw her drinking and smoking like a man he experienced a slight sense of shock. He also guessed that, like Sergeant Swan, her good looks gave her extra confidence, enough to allow her to walk into bars unescorted, to order a drink and sit and wait for him if he was late, and remain quite unperturbed by the men ogling her. He preferred to remain anonymous. He could never leave the force; it provided him with a cloak of the confidence he lacked, offered safe parameters and codes of conduct. He knew exactly where he stood. It also provided companionship.

The programme ended. Helen stubbed out her cigarette and went to the kitchen. 'It won't be long,' she called. Alan soon recognized the aroma of his favourite meal. Helen had introduced him to steak marinated in red wine and garlic and he had been surprised to discover he liked it. Once he had considered garlic as a thing which would never pass his lips. That was the only concession he made to foreign food apart from the odd Italian meal which he suffered for Helen's sake. He opened and poured the wine Helen had placed on the table and felt totally content. 'What are we celebrating?' he asked as she brought the plate in. Fillet steak and wine were not regular items on her shopping list.

'Nothing really. Not exactly celebrating, but I got paid for that job I did a few weeks ago.' She grinned. 'Just thought I'd give you a treat. Might be the last one, I don't think I want to do it any more.'

'That's up to you, sweetheart. We can manage anyway on both our salaries.' He found it hard to get used to the way she spoiled him when she earned a bit extra. It was never like that with his parents; they took a pride in keeping anything extra secret from each other. At times he thought he should show more interest in this sideline of Helen's but it was hardly glamorous, modelling corsetry for the fuller figure. He'd seen the sort of thing in the Sunday supplements and felt it was really a con trick. If someone was gullible enough to believe that by buying the stuff they would attain a figure like Helen's, it was up to them.

'You're beautiful,' he said, 'you really are.'

'Oh, thanks. Steak all right?'

He said it was delicious, unable to understand why she never responded to a compliment, or rather, seemed embarrassed by them. He changed the subject.

'Did you listen to the news? No, forget it, it wouldn't have been on. It might be later, though.'

'No. What news?'

'I don't know all the details yet but an eight-year-old girl was murdered today, out at Little Endesley. I'm afraid it means I'll have to go in tomorrow.'

'Oh, Alan, that's awful.' She looked down at her plate. 'And we're sitting here enjoying good food and wine, with no problems in the world, while her parents must be going through agony.' She put down her knife and fork.

Alan felt a twinge of annoyance and wished he had not mentioned it. She could make herself feel guilty about anything. 'Yes,' he agreed, 'it is awful, but it's happened. You can't take everyone's problems on your shoulders. Come on, now, eat up.'

She cut into her steak. 'Didn't they need you there tonight?'

'No, they had it covered.'

'Well, at least the food didn't go to waste.' She smiled, trying to make amends. The awkward moment had passed. Alan smiled back.

As she lay in bed that night, unable to sleep, despite their gentle lovemaking, she knew it was time to do something. Perhaps she would never overcome her lack of confidence, but her shame was becoming too much to bear. She was giving up her part-time job, that was the first step, but the drinking must also stop. She was a long way from being an alcoholic but she knew she had a problem. And Alan was too good a man to lose.

Helen did not know it, but the death of Sharon Vickers had set the wheels of fate in motion. It was already too late.

4

On that Friday night, a couple of hours before Jacko was picked up and taken to the unit for questioning, he had returned home in a state of shock. Aware that Janet was watching him he was still unable to do more than push his food around the plate. Everything was just as he told Roper and Swan. He had gone up through the woods and marked the trees and was on his way back to the Hall to see if they needed him for anything else that day when he saw it. It was vivid in his mind. His instincts told him to get out as quickly as possible and that's exactly what he did, regardless of the consequences. Even then he knew it was only a matter of time before they came looking for him. They always did. When the police came to his door it was too late.

Janet's face, when she saw the two uniformed officers, said it all. He knew he would lose her this time. When he got back after being questioned he was amazed to see lights burning and windows still open; she must have decided to wait until morning to leave.

Her greeting, when he went in through the back door and found her hand-washing some of her underwear, was icy. He expected that. She made tea without speaking, placed the mugs on the table and said in a voice he did not recognize as hers, 'I want to know, Jacko. I want to know everything – and right now. No more lies, no more pretence.'

So he told her.

When she heard the name Sharon Vickers, Janet felt sick. What she was waiting for had come to pass. Or had it? She listened, for which he was grateful, and what he said had the ring of truth about it. 'What else could I do?' he asked her. 'The police never mentioned no names either, just kept on and on about where I was.'

'If only you'd come straight home, Jacko. They know I don't cover up for you.'

She said she would stick by him but warned him they must not mention the name Sharon Vickers until the whole village was gossiping about it. Not for the first time did she wish she didn't love the man.

On the Saturday morning Janet took the boys and walked down to catch the bus to Rickenham.

The boys always went with her. Brian was too young to be left alone and Michael enjoyed the trip. His reward for helping to carry the groceries was a lurid war comic and sweets. As they walked, Janet sensed the attitude of some of her neighbours even before they spoke. Many of them greeted her normally but some, she knew, thought Jacko was a murderer. Over the years she had become used to the finger of suspicion pointing at her husband but it was still no easier to bear. It was the eventual effect on the boys which worried her most.

It had been two o'clock before she and Jacko had gone to bed the previous night, and she was feeling it now. What he did was wrong, very wrong, but her decision was made and she would stick by it. Now, because of her silence, she was as guilty as he.

By mid-Saturday morning the paperwork was beginning to accumulate. Detective Constable Alan Campbell was busily checking it and devising an easy cross-referencing system for himself. So far, though, no one had come up with a useful lead – or, indeed, any sort of lead.

Ian Roper found it hard to believe that in a place the size of

Little Endesley nothing and no one out of the ordinary had been noticed. He hoped this meant the perpetrator was local; an outsider would surely have been spotted by someone.

Ian thought he might try his own hand at some house-to-house and he took Sergeant Swan along with him to reinterview those who had admitted to being in or near the vicinity at the relevant time. Their first port of call was Mrs Black. She had recovered somewhat from the shock but was still pale and admitted she could not stop shaking. Ian told her it would pass in time. She had nothing new to offer. Her dog had run off and refused to come to heel when she called. Only when she went after it did she realize that what she thought was a bundle of rags left to spoil the countryside by some inconsiderate person was actually the body of a child. 'My eyesight's not what it was. I should wear glasses all the time but they give me a headache. Oh, Inspector, if only I'd gone out earlier like I planned this might never've happened. And to think whoever did it might still have been around.' She wiped away a few tears. 'That poor little mite. I'm sorry, you wanted to know who I saw. Well, there was young Emma Foster and her boyfriend, and Mr Blake. I usually see him, he takes his dog, Beth, out about the same time as me. He was sitting on a log, looking a bit flushed. It was so hot but he will insist Beth gets her proper exercise. I didn't say anything, mind – he keeps himself very much to himself. Just a good afternoon, or a nod of the head. No. That's it, I'm afraid, apart from the children I told you about last night. Three of them, and I don't know who they were. They were way up in the fields laughing and shouting.'

The two teenagers were interviewed together as they both happened to be listening to music in Emma Foster's front room, making the most of her parents' absence.

She and Davey Harrison sat self-consciously side by side on the settee, holding hands and blushing furiously when they were asked about their activities the previous afternoon.

'We told them last night,' Davey said, 'we were just out walking. I can't remember how long we were in the woods, maybe a couple of hours. Some old dear passed us with a dog – '

'Mrs Black,' Emma interrupted. 'My mum knows her. She couldn't have done it.'

'What makes you say that?' Barry Swan asked.

'Well, like I said, she's a friend of my mum's. Anyhow, why would anyone want to do a thing like that?'

'That's what we'd like to find out, Emma. During the time you were in the woods, how far did you go? I mean,' he hastily corrected himself, 'where did you walk exactly?' He had a pretty good idea how far they had gone; his phrasing of the question was less than tactful.

'Up as far as the coppice, then across to the big field – you know, the one with corn or wheat or something in it.'

Barry didn't; his knowledge of rural life was almost non-existent. He could recognize a rose or a tulip, that was about all. However, he knew enough to bet whatever the crop it was high enough to give protection to two nubile young bodies.

'Did you notice anything different about the coppice?'

'No,' Davey replied, puzzled.

'Yes, we did. You remember, I asked you why those orange and white strips were around the trees.'

Davey had obviously had other things on his mind. He shook his head.

'Think carefully, Emma – what time would that have been?'

'Well, they were there on the way up. We left here about quarter past two?' She looked to Davey for confirmation. 'Then we stopped off for some cans of lag . . . Coke and went straight up there.'

Another part of Jacko's alibi was confirmed but they already believed he was not lying about his movements up to two thirty or so on Friday. Earlier on Saturday morning a PC had timed the walk from Jacko's cottage to the coppice. He reported the marked trees. Emma and Davey strolled back about tea-time on Friday, stopped to chat to a couple of friends then returned to their respective homes. They were at the stage of courtship where they only had eyes for each other.

The third call that morning brought unexpected results and what might turn out to be a lead.

Harry Morgan lived in one of the cottages in the square. His tiny front garden was a blaze of colour; hanging baskets, full of blue and white lobelia and multi-coloured impatiens, were suspended dangerously low, in Ian's opinion, from numerous wrought-iron hooks. The effect was dazzling. Barry pushed the bell and grinned sickly when it chimed the opening bars of 'There's No Place Like Home'.

The man who answered the door was in his middle years, blond hair thinning and his body running fat. Otherwise he was immaculately turned out. Under his left arm he carried a miniature poodle.

'Yes?' he said, his eyes narrowing suspiciously.

They produced their identity. 'Mr Harold Morgan?'

'They said last night someone'd be back,' Morgan commented ungraciously. 'I can't tell you any more than I told them.'

It was even hotter than yesterday. It was not yet noon but the two men on the doorstep felt the sun beating down on their heads. The tarmac on the road was sticky and imprinted with tyre marks, but Harry Morgan, who had spent the morning in the shaded cool of his cottage, was sweating from the moment he opened the door.

'May we come in for a few minutes? Might be a little more private, don't you think?'

Sullenly Morgan stood aside to let them in. The interior was small, too small for three men to crowd into the hallway, and impeccably decorated if, in Ian's opinion, a little effeminate. Flower-sprigged paper covered the walls, the carpet was rose pink to match, and a vase of tea roses, nearly past their best, scattered a few sweet-smelling petals over the half-moon table on which it rested. There were only two rooms downstairs: the kitchen at the back where bright primrose and white paint and tiles could be seen through the open door, and the room into which they were shown.

Harry Morgan did not invite them to occupy the chintz-covered chairs, nor did he take one himself. The dog remained

44

passively under his arm. Detective Chief Inspector Roper took in the room at a glance. No television, sumptuous comfort and plenty of books, not paperbacks either.

'You've come again about the child, I suppose?' Morgan volunteered when his unwelcome guests remained silent.

'Last night you told one of my men you were in the woods at some period yesterday afternoon – is that correct?' The Chief was vaguely irritated by the man. It was irrational, but it happened from time to time.

'Yes. I take Suki up there if the weather is hot. She doesn't need much exercise, do you, my pet?' He fondled Suki's woolly head. 'I carry her most of the way so she doesn't get too hot then I let her run free. It's cooler, you see, under the trees.'

Good God, Ian thought, and they talk about a dog's life. 'What time was this?'

'I've already said, I don't know exactly.' Morgan's eyes wandered across the room and rested on the cupboard doors of a Welsh dresser which stood in the chimney recess. For some reason he was very nervous. 'I tried to remember last night, but they took me by surprise, knocking on my door so late.'

'It was hardly the small hours, sir,' Barry said defensively. 'About nine thirty, I believe.'

Morgan chose to ignore the remark. 'I know it wasn't before three because I was listening to music on the radio. Mozart. My particular favourite. Then I did a few bits around the house. I can't really say, probably fourish.'

'And the time you returned?'

'Ah, that's easy. It was five thirty.'

'How can you be so certain?'

'Because I called in at the post office for the *Rickenham Herald* and Mrs Spencer said I was lucky there were any left. She was pushing the sun blind up ready to close when I arrived.' Morgan made the briefest of eye contact with the Chief, knowing this could be verified, before his eyes slid back to the dresser.

'Now you've had time to think about it, can you remember anything out of the ordinary?'

'No. I only saw a young couple and they were so busy

45

cuddling and kissing I don't suppose they even noticed Suki and me. Look, I went through all this last night, I don't know anything more about it.'

'Do you work, Mr Morgan?'

The question took him by surprise. 'Of course I do.'

'But you were not at work yesterday afternoon.'

'Oh, I see what you're getting at. No, Inspector, or whoever you are. I'm on a week's leave. You can check with my firm if you so wish.'

'That may not be necessary,' the Chief told him, 'but we'll make a note of the name and address, if you've no objection.'

Morgan walked towards the dresser and opened one of the drawers. As he did so he nudged the cupboard beneath it with his knee, a barely visible movement, to make sure it was shut. From the drawer he produced a card and handed it to Ian. On it was his name in large, black fancy lettering, followed by the name and address of the firm.

'You're a chartered accountant?'

'It says so there, doesn't it? I've worked for Bleasedale & Co. for twenty-seven years and I'm sure they'll tell you both my work and my own person are well respected.'

Pompous, Ian thought. Ridiculous, pompous little man.

'Now, if there's nothing else, gentlemen, I have things to do.'

'No. There's nothing else for the moment. Thank you for your time. If you should recall anything, please get in touch. Here's my card, or you can speak to whoever's in the mobile unit at any time.'

'That thing out there?' Morgan looked towards the window but like a reflex action, his eyes flickered back across the room. There was no reason for asking the question, except for the man's excessive nervousness, but Ian had a familiar feeling in the pit of his stomach.

'Is there, by any chance, something in that cupboard you don't wish us to know about, Mr Morgan?'

'No. No, of course there isn't.' But the involuntary backward step he took confirmed there was.

'Then you have no objection to showing us?' It was another

chance. Morgan could refuse – but this was a murder investigation, and if they went off to get a warrant, whatever was in there would have disappeared. 'An innocent child has been killed, and if you are what you say you are, a man with nothing to hide, you have nothing to fear.'

Even someone who lived without a television set and had a penchant for French literature and Mozart must be aware that he could refuse. But he didn't. As if the strength had left his legs, Morgan crumpled into an armchair. 'Go ahead. It had to happen sometime.' He mopped his brow with a crisp, white handkerchief. Suki, clutched tightly beneath his arm, began to yap.

Ian motioned for Barry to go ahead; they asked each other with their eyes whether this was too good to be true. What was in there? Some article belonging to Sharon? No, her father had said nothing was missing.

Barry stepped across to the dresser and pulled open the doors, giving a whistle of surprise when he saw what was contained there. The titles of the neat stacks of videos were explicit enough for him not to have to ask what sort of entertainment they provided.

'I couldn't help it,' Morgan told them, almost in tears, 'after my wife died, even before, really, when she was ill for such a long time. I was never unfaithful to her, it wasn't in me, but I needed something. If they ever find out at work I'm finished.' He blew his nose noisily. 'Whatever must you think of me?' There was no real answer to that.

'Where did you get them?'

Morgan shuddered. 'I'd rather not say. Just arrest me if you're going to, just get it over with.'

'Why should we arrest you?'

'It's illegal, isn't it? That sort of thing? That . . . that filth.' He spat the word, his self-disgust obvious, but he was less cowed; this was what he had feared, not the investigation into the child's death.

'Not necessarily. It depends what they contain. Such things can be hired from video shops all over the country nowadays.

However, we will have to take them away to check they don't contravene the pornography laws.' Suddenly Ian realized what was puzzling him. 'You said these are for your own use, Mr Morgan – how do you watch them?'

'How do I watch them? The recording machine, on the television, of course. Oh, I see. The TV's upstairs, in the bedroom. We didn't always have one but when my wife became bedridden, I bought it for her. When she was too weak to read she'd lie and watch films.'

'Hmm. Do you have a couple of carrier bags? It might be less embarrassing for you if we're not seen carrying these away with us.'

Morgan rose, still clutching the dog, and went out to the kitchen.

Ian and Barry were well aware that the tapes might contain nothing more sinister than the usual acres of naked flesh grinding away with monotonous regularity. If so, and if they proved to have come from a harmless source, and if they were only used for Morgan's personal entertainment, they might decide to return them. With so much foreign stuff coming into the country it would take the whole of the police force just to confiscate the damn things. They tended to be lenient – they didn't have much choice. But if the tapes were part of a load they were looking for, originating in London and distributed recently throughout East Anglia, in which sex between consenting adults was not enough to satisfy the viewer, it would be a different story.

The Chief decided not to question Morgan further for the moment. He was already weak and terrified. It would be easy to get him to divulge their source once they'd been examined. A sleepless night and he'd tell them anything they needed to know.

'Don't forget to call me if you recall anything about yesterday.' Morgan would rack his brains to come up with something to score a few Brownie points now.

They left, carrying the tapes in a couple of plastic bags,

48

stopped to pick up reports from the unit and headed towards Rickenham.

'Not going to see Blake, sir?'

'Not just yet. Robbins and Davies'll be back there this morning. Maybe later. Davies tells me he was seen hanging around the village school a couple of years ago. He knows the man, I'll let him have first crack.'

The hedges were thick with foliage and the air was still. The drone of an early combine harvester was the only sound. They passed just two people, a man and a woman, looking hot and sweaty, their gaily coloured rucksacks strapped across their backs. The midday heat was oppressive. The Chief's car, though comfortable, was too old to have anything approaching air-conditioning. Both front windows were wound right down but instead of creating a cooling breeze this merely allowed the sun to beat in. They were not sorry to be back in the town.

Pushing through the gleaming glass swing doors they stepped into the welcome coolness of the modern reception area, the one redeeming feature, Ian thought, of the new building. In the winter there was central heating which was actually effective, unlike the old, ridged radiators which were fine if you sat on them, but otherwise useless, and in the summer, on the few days like today, air-conditioning as chilling as anything in the United States. Apart from this he'd move back to the old HQ at the drop of a hat. He hated the anonymity of steel and glass and polished floors, the no-smoking areas, even though he'd given up again. It did not have the familiar smell of a police station – at least, not yet. Maybe in time the odours of sweat, damp, fags and fear would permeate the walls and make it home, but it would take years.

They took the stairs to the first floor, a discipline the Chief adhered to in deference to his waistline, or so he said. Moira, who constantly told him he should take more exercise, was probably the only one who knew that as a boy of ten he had been trapped in a lift, the old-fashioned sort, with two sliding grilles where the wall could be seen flashing past. He thanked

49

his lucky stars he had not been born in New York or some other city with skycrapers – he would have been in a constant state of trepidation. Barry, whose shirt was sticking to him, knew better than to suggest the lift.

They dumped the carrier bags on the floor of the room set aside for major inquiries and put the paperwork on the table.

'What are we going to do with this lot, sir? We ought to get someone to have a look fairly sharpish.'

'I agree, but tea first. Sort it out, will you?'

Barry picked up the internal phone and pressed three digits, requesting a tray of tea for two to be sent to the Chief's office. Ian sat with his elbow on the desk, his thumb under his chin and his index finger resting on his cheekbone. It was a pose he unconsciously adopted when he was deep in thought.

'If it is child pornography, it might be a vital link. I mean, supposing these are home-made – Morgan or someone he knows gets hold of the Vickers girl and – I don't know, bribes her? Or threatens her? Then loses his nerve, afraid she'll talk, and kills her. Does that sound far-fetched? Everyone we've spoken to so far says she wasn't like other kids her age. Could it be because of what she's done?'

'I know, but Doc Harris said – '

'I know what the Doc said, no sexual interference as far as he could tell. The post-mortem'll tell us for sure. But you know as well as I that vaginal penetration isn't the only way. God, what a mess.' Ian picked up the telephone receiver and snapped some instructions into it. 'OK,' he said, 'send whoever's free. What? Oh good, tell them well done.' He replaced the receiver.

'Markham and Finch are the glory boys today. They've finally picked up the lads who've been passing off the dud tenners *and* persuaded them to say where they came from. Knowing Markham, I wouldn't like to hear the details of how they were persuaded.'

There was a knock at the door. A uniformed PC entered and placed the tray on the desk. Barry looked surprised. 'I was in the canteen anyway, sir – thought I'd save WPC Robbins the trip.' And WPC Robbins, Barry guessed, would have been more than pleased at her colleague's attitude regarding equality of the sexes.

Almost immediately Detective Constable Campbell arrived in response to the Chief's call.

'Come in, have a seat.'

Alan did so. 'Have we got a break, sir?'

'I'm not sure. It's probably run-of-the-mill, but I'd like you to have a look at this lot.' He picked up one of the carrier bags and held it open so Alan could see the contents. 'You won't get through them all by yourself, it'll take ages, but I'm sure there won't be a lack of volunteers to help.'

'Porn, sir?'

'Porn indeed. Might simply be a man's harmless hobby, but we've got to check.'

'All of them?'

'All of them. Start by picking out a few at random. You might not have to go through the whole of each one. If they're what we're looking for it'll be obvious, but I don't want any missed, it could turn out to be important. Do you have a photo of Sharon Vickers? Good. Then if there's any sign of a child you stop the thing and have a damned good look. OK, Campbell, that's all.' Alan left, taking the carrier bags with him.

'And now,' Ian said, 'back to Sharon Vickers. Motive? Any ideas?'

'I suppose we have to start with Jacko. Maybe he tried a bit too hard this time. As you say, she was no ordinary eight-year-old. Perhaps she screamed or fought and he panicked.' Barry consulted the notes he had taken the previous evening when he spoke to his counterpart in the West Country. 'Except there's no history of violence, not even in his younger days. Several incidents down there concerning young girls, same as here. He had to leave in the end because of continuing threats against himself and his wife. Again, his form's the same as here – exposed himself, made one or two attempts to get the girls to touch him, no more than that. One or two incidents reported later, after he left the area, but none of the kids seems terribly alarmed. He swore them to secrecy, and kids that age thrive on secrets although they often confided to their best friend. It was usually the best friend who told an adult. That's mostly how he was caught.'

'Missing children? Unsolved murders in Cornwall? Anything along those lines?'

'Not a thing, or nothing that can be connected to Jacko. They ran it through their computers for us. I think we've drawn a blank there, sir. He's no other form, not so much as the proverbial parking ticket.'

'What makes someone kill a child, Barry? Adults, bad as it is, I can occasionally understand. Driven to it by years of nagging or adultery, things like that. But a child?'

Barry knew the Chief was working himself into the frame of mind necessary to carry out the investigation. When he first joined the Rickenham force Sergeant Baker, an old hand at the game, had told him the Chief only used first names when he was keyed up, when he was trying to form a close-knit team to tackle a problem. Once the case was solved he reverted to rank or no appellation at all. Only with a few men, those of equal rank and above, was the reverse permitted. This was known and accepted by all who worked under him. Yet he managed to keep the balance between friendly support and over-familiarity just right. 'What sort of a sick mind are we looking for?' Ian absent-mindedly patted his shirt pocket but did not feel the comforting bulge of a cigarette packet, forgetting, as he often did, that he had given up again. Barry did not offer him one. He did not want to be the one to take the blame if the Chief took it up again, but it meant he had to forgo the pleasure himself.

'Another child?' Barry suggested. 'It wouldn't be the first time.'

'It's possible, especially as she mixed with older children, when she mixed at all, that is. There's no secondary school in Little Endesley but she would have known most of the kids who attend schools in Rickenham.' Ian looked at his watch. 'Doc Harris should have something for us by now.'

He asked to be put through to the mortuary and after a brief conversation told Barry what he had learned. The Doc, as he was generally known, had little to report. The cause of death was asphyxiation, the time of death between three and four p.m. on Friday. No sexual interference, not yesterday, not ever. There were no items of clothing missing, even her hair ribbon was still in place, which wiped out Barry's theory: this would not have been the case if there had been any sort of struggle. The dog hairs on her clothing proved to have come from Mrs Black's golden retriever. 'It's a bloody mystery,' Doc Harris told the Chief.

'And,' Ian said when he finished relating these facts to Barry, 'it's no bloody use at all.' This was stated with far more vehemence than was usual for the Chief.

'The whole thing's impossible. John Cotton didn't come up with anything either, and there's no one better than him at scene-of-crime. How can it happen and no clues whatever be discovered?'

The question, Barry guessed, was rhetorical. If he could have answered it he would be able to solve the case. John Cotton, head of scene-of-crime investigations, left no stone unturned. Literally. The area around Sharon's body had been taped off and the ground surrounding her gone over with a fine-tooth comb. John himself had undertaken the searching of the first few feet so there was as little disturbance as possible. Not a number ten boot in sight. He found nothing but a couple of dog-ends which had been lying there far too long to have any relevance to the crime. A wider circle was made, and so on, until it fanned out for almost half a mile in diameter. After that men walked in lines and made a general search of the whole woods. Empty drink cans, sweet wrappers and one or two strands of fabric caught on tree trunks or fallen logs were collected and put into plastic bags. They would be catalogued, fingerprinted and analysed. But unless they came up with something with which to match them it seemed a pointless exercise. And worse. It had not rained for several weeks so even in the shade the ground was too hard to retain a footprint.

The Chief was thinking. Barry fingered his cigarette packet

and wondered whether he dared chance it. During the hour or so before he slept last night he had racked his brains to come up with something. He was ambitious; recently promoted to sergeant, he was already anxious to take the next step up the ladder. What he needed was to break a case such as this one. Nothing had come to mind. And there was Lucy.

On Friday morning he'd gone into a branch of the bank he used, partly with the intention of drawing some cash but also to ask her if she'd like to have a drink with him. He'd fancied Lucy for some time and had decided to do something about it. She'd said yes, as he'd expected. Girls rarely turned him down. WPC Judy Robbins, Lucy's best friend, had learned of this date and laughed at Barry, pointing out that Lucy was not the type to jump into bed with anyone, especially the likes of him. Judy was one of the few females he did not fancy, not because of her looks but because she was totally impervious to his charms. She frequently told him he was vain, arrogant and patronizing, which he was but couldn't see. Barry was determined to prove her wrong; Lucy, like many before her, would succumb.

Firstly, because of having to go out to Little Endesley, Barry had had to telephone and postpone the arranged time of meeting. When he finished on Friday night there had only been enough time to dash into the nearest Indian restaurant, which fortunately served both wine and lager. Secondly, when Lucy agreed to go back to his place for a nightcap, he had realized he wouldn't be able to cut the mustard. He did not even try, it would have been too humiliating. He feigned gentlemanly conduct, saying how he liked to get to know a girl properly, etc. Lucy was rather sceptical. Apart from what Judy had told her, he didn't strike her that way. He had offered to drive her home but she refused and got a cab instead.

So, Barry told himself, he was not quite the stud he imagined after all. He could not bring himself to tell her the true reason and he was not perceptive enough to realize how much more she would have thought of him if he had.

Barry knew that the fault, if it could be so called, lay with Sharon Vickers. It was a feeling alien to him, but he knew he

54

would in some way be degrading himself if he indulged in sex whilst the little girl's body lay cold on a mortuary slab. Maybe he was human after all.

So far he had not seen Judy Robbins today, and was pleased he did not have to witness her smug smile, very pleased it was not her who'd brought up the tray of tea.

'Here,' the Chief said, 'you start with these.' Barry pulled himself back to the present and took the file he was handed. For the next hour or so they went over the statements that were steadily coming in.

For the second night in a row Ian Roper returned home much later than he would have liked and wished that Moira was there. She could not help him solve the case but her presence was always a comfort. Perhaps he should tell her so more often. He could talk to her; she was an astute woman. Occasionally she voiced an opinion which helped to throw a different light on some aspect of a case. Why did she have to be away right now? He looked at the time and decided to ring her anyway.

Moira went to bed early when she was at her mother's as the lady in question had a tendency to believe that those who rose after six thirty in the morning were idlers and layabouts. Before he could place his briefcase under the hall table and his keys on top of it, the telephone rang. Moira had beaten him to it.

'Are you coping? I heard on the ten o'clock news. Oh, Ian, her poor parents.'

Of course, it would be public knowledge by now. Mostly it was Ian's duty to prepare the bland, standard press and media statements which were issued after the victim's relatives had been informed, but there had been a memo on his desk that morning saying that Detective Superintendent Ross had done the necessary. DC Alan Campbell was wrong when he told his wife she might hear the news on Friday night. His superiors thought it more politic to leave the masses uninformed until the following day. Ian prayed Ross's interest would go no further than that. They were not, and never would be, on friendly terms. Ross was dictatorial and took no account of the feelings or needs of those under him. He expected his men to perform like robots, to go by the book in any given situation. Perhaps the weather would hold and Ross would take his unlovely, unlovable hide off to the golf course where he could annoy Doc Harris for most of Sunday morning.

'What did it say? The news items?'

'Oh the usual thing, not very much. Just the girl's name and age and the whereabouts of the murder, then the number to ring for anyone with information. You know the sort of thing.' Of course he knew, for heaven's sake. He was a policeman, did the woman think he was stupid? And then, recalling the words of Brian Lord, the once-hated police psychologist whose lecture he'd been 'requested' to attend, he calmed down and asked how she was enjoying herself. He patiently listened to stories about the beach and a meal at a fish restaurant which the boys loved because they were allowed wine. 'Mother's treat,' Moira hastily amended in case Ian thought she had been extravagant. Sensing his distraction and knowing she would have to bear with it until the case was over, she gave him her own and Mark's love, reminded him of their train time and hung up.

Ian went through to the kitchen of 14 Belmont Terrace, the three-bedroomed house they had saved hard for, and counted his blessings. While he made coffee and a doorstep sandwich he sipped a stiff whisky and water. 'I keep forgetting,' he told himself. He was thinking about the lecture and the promises he made himself at the time. Promises to give as much attention to his family as he did the job, to have time for himself too. He did not want his marriage to become another statistic, one broken by the stress of the job.

He finished the whisky and poured another. He deserved it. The kettle switched itself off and the coffee was forgotten. He bit into the badly made sandwich, crumbs falling on to the breadboard from which he ate it, and tried to concentrate on the local paper. The *Rickenham Herald* came out on Fridays and therefore did not contain the story of Sharon Vickers' death. It was in the shops first thing Friday morning so the editor,

Martyn Bright, was thwarted: it was too late even for a few lines in the Stop Press column on the front page. Ian had not got around to reading it the previous evening; tiredness had overtaken him. Now he was in the mood for it. The trivia that was reported never ceased to amaze him, although the rag was good value for money. The advertisements of numerous estate agents paid for its publication. Here and there he spotted familiar names, old lags and local villains whose cases had come before the magistrates. Ian suspected the *Herald* had a full-time man at the courts: if so much as a pair of bicycle clips went missing the population of Rickenham Green would read about it at the weekend. There was his own professional interest too. He, or someone at the station, dealt with the paper on a daily basis. They had an agreement. They, the police, would pass on all relevant information if Martyn Bright did not harass or pester them. Bright was young and brash and, despite his humble Suffolk origins, contrived to speak with a mid-Atlantic accent, much, Ian thought, like the Radio One disc jockeys whose raucous tones enamated from his son's bedroom on the rare occasions he was at home. To listen to Bright, one would think he was head of one of the nationals. Unfortunately, the news of the return of Joe Bloggs' bicycle clips was hardly likely to be flashed across the international syndicate.

It had worked, though. Reading about other people's problems, small maybe, but important to them, took his mind temporarily off the case. Too much concentrated thinking and Ian knew he was capable of missing the wood for the trees. One more whisky, then bed. Tomorrow, no matter what, he would treat himself to a decent meal, not one of Moira's from the freezer, good though they were, and not from a take-away. Then he remembered. Tomorrow she'd be home. And there were four meals uneaten.

He stayed up only to watch the local news headlines, which gave brief details of the murder.

5

The police left Jacko alone on Saturday. They were too engrossed in the rest of the village. At least he had not been arrested. Not yet.

He went up to Endesley Hall hoping to see his boss as there were a few things he wanted to clear up before Monday – or his arrest, whichever came first. If he still had a job, that is. One of his chores was to replace some loose bricks in a gatepost into which Eileen Butterfield had carelessly reversed her Mini whilst trying to turn around in too small a space.

Jacko did not work fixed hours. Sometimes he took time off in the week and repaid it on a Saturday or Sunday. There was no real reason for his presence at the hall today, he simply wanted to find out how he stood with his employer.

Gerald Langdon happened to be in the drive with his two children when Jacko arrived. They were on their way to the swimming baths in Rickenham, thus giving Sonia a few well-earned hours on her own, unimpeded by her boisterous sons. Gerald's office was quiet at the moment but he was still tempted to go in and look at the post. He was aware that he was in danger of becoming a workaholic and made a conscious decision not to leave the boys in the pool whilst he did so. He would join them, the exercise would do him good. He also volunteered to do the shopping, a kindness appreciated by his wife, but one which also filled her with consternation. Although she wrote out a list of things she needed from Fine Fare she knew many of the items he brought back would bear little resemblance to those she wanted.

It was almost ten o'clock. Jacko had waited until Janet and the boys set off for the bus stop before he left the cottage. Still not totally convinced she would stay with him, he wanted to make sure she took nothing other than her shopping bags with her. Satisfied, he made his way slowly up to the Hall, uncertain what his reception would be. Mr Langdon had already put up with enough trouble.

'Here's the keys, Peter – you and David wait in the car,' Gerald told them when he saw Jacko approach. The boys did as they were bade, scattering gravel as they raced towards the vehicle.

'Morning, Jacko.'

'Good morning, Mr Langdon. I've come to fix that post.' Jacko's head was bowed, his cap, literally and metaphorically, in his hand.

'Fine, go ahead, but there was no hurry.' Gerald looked uncomfortable. So he was to get the sack after all. 'The police were here last night.'

'I guessed they would be.'

'They spoke to both myself and Sonia. We told them the truth, what time you were here and when we last saw you.'

'Yes.' Jacko was wringing his cap between his hands. Gerald had an urge to snatch it from him.

'We couldn't pretend you were here when you weren't, you know.'

'No.'

'Look, Jacko, is there anything in it? I mean . . .' But he didn't really know what he meant. You could hardly ask someone if they went around killing children. He wanted to help, maybe get him a good defence lawyer. Gerald's own work was mainly dealing with personal injury claims so he could not do it adequately himself. Would he want to anyway, if Jacko were guilty? He was not sure.

'No, Mr Langdon, I never done nothing.' Gerald ignored the double negative, he knew what he meant. 'But I . . .'

59

'Yes?'

'Nothing. Honest. I never touched her. Will you want me to be leaving, then? I'd understand, you know, after everything.' He was almost in tears.

'No, you don't have to leave. If you're telling the truth, and I believe you are, it'll only make things look worse for you and, if you're not, well, you'll be forced to leave at some point.' Gerald coughed. He felt awkward and embarrassed. Dealing with insurance companies he was a ruthless opponent but face to face with his staff, both at home and in the office, he suffered from pangs of inadequacy. This was because he was one of that rare breed who truly believe all men are equal and he felt guilty for being in a position of being able to afford to pay them. The logical side of his brain recognized that if it wasn't for this employment several families would not be in such a sound financial position. This did not make the present situation any easier.

'Thank you, Mr Langdon. In that case I'd best be getting on with it.' He indicated the small, brick gatepost with a nod of his head.

'OK, Jacko, but you can leave it until Monday if you'd rather.'

'No, I'm here now, I may as well see to it.'

Gerald got into his car, much to the relief of his impatient sons and the man to whom he'd been talking. He thought it over on the drive to the baths but could not convince himself Jacko was the culprit.

By midday Jacko's task was completed. He cleaned his tools and locked them in the shed, hanging the key in its rightful place in the back porch of the Hall. Then he went home. He was not a religious man but he found himself making bargains with God. If Janet and the boys returned to him he would never, no matter how great the temptation, even think of small girls again, let alone expose himself to them.

Despite her reassurances, Janet was aware of her husband's fears. He was not a man able to hide his feelings; even the awful things he did he felt compelled to confess to her. This morning she had witnessed his anxiety in the way his eyes followed her around the kitchen as she prepared breakfast for the four of them. Brian and Michael were unaware anything was wrong.

Once she was sure the boys were presentable enough for the trip into town they had set off to catch the bus. Janet carried her handbag and some empty carriers. Still not entirely satisfied, Jacko had checked the old tea caddy on the kitchen shelf which held money for the milkman. It was still there. With a slight uplift in spirit, he had then left himself.

Janet did not see anyone she knew in the supermarket, which was unusual but also a relief. Many of her neighbours came into town on Saturdays but not always on the early bus. The girl on the check-out was familiar though. She lived in the village. Her name was Denise something or other and her mother helped out at the post office.

The queue at Denise's till was the shortest so Janet joined it.

'Hello, Mrs Penhaligon. I didn't expect to see you here today.' She meant no malice – her intentions were, in fact, the opposite – but she was a stupid girl. In trying to show Janet she bore no ill feelings, whatever her husband may have done, she said the first tactless thing which came into her head.

Janet's purse was in her hand; she was pulling out three ten-pound notes with which to pay.

'Oh?' she asked, the words only just registering. 'Why not?'

'Because of . . . well, you know, because of what your husband's gone and done. We couldn't believe it, me and mum. Of course, we knew all about the other thing, but really.' Denise did not understand that Janet loved her husband, that any pain he felt, so did she.

The neon lights blurred, the sound of talking and rattling trolleys became a wave of indistinguishable noise, swelling and fading. For reasons Janet couldn't comprehend the supermarket floor came up towards her. Before her head hit something hard and sharp she heard a quick scream and vaguely thought it might have come from one of the boys.

Tom and Julie Vickers had not gone to bed on that Friday night but sat in stunned silence in their front room. On Saturday morning they gave detailed statements to the police.

Tom said he was at work all day on Friday, had not left his office even at lunchtime but remained there to eat the sandwiches Julie had made for him, washing them down with a couple of cups of coffee he made with his own kettle. He worked for a large property developing company, one which was still surviving the recession, although there was talk of redundancies. There had been recent cutbacks in expenditure. Fortunately for the Vickers family, any redundancies in the foreseeable future would be made amongst the labour force. Tom's job was the drawing up of plans from specifications set out for him by qualified architects. His salary was adequate enough to pay for the mortgage on the house, to feed and clothe his family, to cover a night out once a week and to save for an annual holiday. He considered himself a lucky man.

Before their marriage Julie worked as a hairdresser in Rickenham; now, although Tom was not keen on her continuing to work, she earned a useful weekly sum setting or perming the grey heads of the older generation in the village in the comfort of their own homes. This suited her perfectly. It gave her a measure of independence and got her out of the house. During the school holidays the children either came with her or, more often than not, went off to play with friends. They had moved from Rickenham when Sharon was on the way, wanting a more rural atmosphere in which to bring up their children.

On Friday Julie cooked a meal for Ronnie and Sharon at lunchtime. She and Tom were going out in the evening and she planned to give them sandwiches and cake for their tea, or something on toast if they preferred. Just before two a couple of Ronnie's friends knocked on the back door and asked if he was coming out. Sharon went with them.

'Did she often do that, Mrs Vickers? Go off with her brother?'
It was WPC Livingstone who asked the question. There was
more than one case of a jealous child killing a sibling. There
were also recorded cases where it had been an accident, a
dangerous game gone wrong.

'Oh, yes, quite often. She hardly ever played with girls.
Ronnie didn't seem to mind her tagging along. Other times
she'd go off by herself. I know she's only . . . Oh, God.' Julie
Vickers lit the fourth cigarette of the interview. It seemed to be
a way to stop the pain. She inhaled deeply. 'She was my
daughter, I know, but she was special. Not like other kids. She
knew where she was allowed to go and she stuck with what we
told her. She was way ahead of the others in school, well above
average. She wouldn't go off with a stranger, not Sharon.' Julie
paused. 'She wrote poetry, you know.' Julie's face softened at
the recollection.

Pat Livingstone asked if she might look at some, and to save
Mrs Vickers trouble, said she would go with her to Sharon's
room. It was a tactful way of following procedure. The girl's
bedroom needed to be searched – it might hold a clue as to who
killed her. They went upstairs together.

Nothing sinister came to light. True, there were books rather
than dolls lining the shelves but there was a large teddy bear on
the bed. It was a tidy room but not obsessively so. Scattered
around were odd-shaped bits of local flint-stones, games and a
few items of clothing. Pat turned the pages of the red exercise
book she was handed and read what Sharon had written. There
was nothing. No signs of fear or apprehension, just childish
doggerel which, considering her age, showed what good insight
she possessed concerning her family and friends. No one who
penned the amusing words on those pages could have been
unhappy. Even Pat Livingstone, who had been there at the
gruesome Robertson case in Ipswich, felt tears prick the back of
her eyelids as she tried to picture the sturdy, attractive little girl
she'd seen only in death, sitting on her bed writing those lines.
She handed back the book and thanked Mrs Vickers.

They returned to the front room, Pat once more composed.

'And after they went out?'

'I washed up and left everything ready for later. Tom and I go out most Fridays. Sally, that's my neighbour's daughter, babysits. We'd booked a table at Salvatore's.'

Pat knew the place. It was the best of the three Italian restaurants in Rickenham. There was the one by the bridge, overpriced, but where people liked to be seen, a pizza and pasta house which was more up-market than the chain pizza parlours, and Salvatore's, which served good food at reasonable prices. She had only been there once but had vowed to return, next time with a different companion from the one who shared her first meal. Out of loneliness she had accepted an offer from one of her fellow PCs and finished the evening by wondering if she was becoming a terrible snob. Sandy Wilkson, now thankfully transferred, demanded chips with his meal. Politely he was told they served sauté potatoes with the veal and these, to the management's horror, he smothered with tomato sauce, albeit their home-made variety begrudgingly brought from the kitchen in a sauce boat. He did not ask her if she preferred wine but ordered two lagers. In bed that night she questioned herself. If the man was prepared to take her out and pay for their food, did it matter so much if he wanted chips? Why shouldn't he have them? And why did minor incidents like this embarrass her so?

'And why,' she wondered as she sat in the Vickers' front room, 'am I thinking about such trivialities at a time like this? This poor woman has lost her child. Sharon Vickers is dead, she no longer has the chance to be embarrassed. What on earth is the matter with me?' And with that salutary self-admonishment WPC Livingstone pushed the crippling loneliness she managed to conceal with her efficiency and fearlessness to the back of her mind and got on with the job in hand.

Detective Chief Inspector Roper had picked her for this interview because of those very two qualities, and because she was female. There was another officer with her, there had to be if she was to take formal statements, but he remained in the background, mostly taking notes.

Julie Vickers had kissed her children goodbye, smiling to herself as Ronnie rubbed his face as if he could remove that offensive gesture from the eyes of his friends, and never saw her daughter again.

'About twenty past two I walked up to Miss Morris's to do her perm. I got back here about four.'

'What time were you expecting Ronnie and Sharon back?'

'No later than six. It's not really late, is it? It's not dark for ages after that.' Pat saw how desperate she was for reassurance that it was not her fault.

'No, not late at all. What time did Ronnie get back?'

'About ten to. He knew we were going out. They both did. They're good kids, they've both got watches and they're rarely late.'

'And you, Mr Vickers?'

'I got in about twenty minutes after Ronnie, about ten past six. I finish at five thirty. By the time I got to the car and drove through Rickenham a good twenty-five minutes must have elapsed. It's terrible on Fridays.'

Tom Vickers' statement was verified. He did not leave the office all day and those extra minutes were accounted for by a hold-up at the new roundabout by Fine Fare. Built with the opposite effect in mind, it simply made matters worse. It was a shambles on late-night shopping days when cars queued to get into the multi-storey car-park and blocked off two exits.

'And then . . .' Julie said, 'and then . . .' but she could not continue. She was shaking from head to foot, but her eyes were cold and hard. Still she had shed no tears. Yet it was not towards her husband she moved in search of comfort, but to Pat Livingstone, who put an awkward arm around her shoulders, gaining comfort herself from contact with another human being. The 'and then' was the arrival of Sergeant Davies, their friendly village copper, who could not be bringing bad news. Except it was half-past six and Sharon had not come home. And Julie had shouted at Ronnie, shouted, not because she was particularly worried at that time but because, selfishly, she wanted to have a bath and get ready to go out. But Sharon was already dead. She had not even sensed anything was wrong. What kind of a mother was she? It was not Ronnie's fault. He was ten years old, sensible enough, but his sister was not his responsibility. She had not so much as told him to look after her. Besides, at times, Sharon seemed the elder of the two.

'And we didn't cancel our table,' Julie said, heaping more guilt on to her shoulders, trying to concentrate on small things, anything other than the awful truth.

WPC Livingstone and PC Palmer left the Vickers to their grief and went to see that their statements were typed up. Ronnie would be questioned separately, as would all the children in the village. Sharon's form teacher and the headmistress of the school must also be seen – perhaps there was bullying, perhaps they, who must have known her well, would provide one more piece of the jigsaw. Another name on their list was Michael Penhaligon.

Every individual within a three-mile radius of Little Endesley was eventually interviewed. Press coverage ensured that they were all aware of the reason for the questions but it also activated the usual percentage of cranks: the people who telephoned or wrote or turned up at the station to say that either they were the murderer or they knew who the murderer was. They had to be listened to. It was time-consuming but each report was recorded and checked. What fools the police would look if one of them was telling the truth.

Harold Morgan remained at home for the remainder of Saturday, too ashamed to show his face. Quite wrongly, he felt sure everyone knew what those carrier bags contained. His neighbours, however, thought him to be a respectable business-man who, like themselves, had received a routine visit from the police.

His normally too healthy appetite disappeared and he forced himself to eat the meagre meal he knocked together from the contents of the freezer. Even the runner beans he grew with fastidious care and enjoyed so much lay wilting on the draining board. The death of the child meant nothing to him. He and his wife were childless, out of choice, and had turned each other into substitutes. Now Gladys was dead, Suki took her place. What mattered more than anything to Harold Morgan was his reputation. That was far more important than some snivelling child.

George Blake had been in bed when he received a visit on Friday night. His heart thudded. No one visited him in the daytime, let alone at night. It could only mean one thing – trouble. He opened the door the length of the security chain and, seeing this was no social call, clutched tightly at the neck of his woollen dressing-gown. He took a deep breath, pushed the door closed and released the chain. The police officers on his doorstep were polite and did not detain him long. They apologized for disturbing him but said that as his upstairs light was on they did not think he was asleep. George Blake confirmed he had been in the woods that afternoon with his dog, Beth, just as he had been every other day of the year, winter or summer. He had walked her up to the big field then let her run loose. He had seen Mrs Black and a couple of kids. No, he could not say who they were, nor could he describe them. He was given the night to think it over. If those children had been Ronnie and his friends, and maybe Sharon, his statement could be vital.

He received his second visit on Saturday morning as he was putting the lead on Beth with the intention of going to the post office for a few bits and pieces. He didn't like doing that, he preferred to go into to Rickenham once or twice a week and shop anonymously, where the village gossips couldn't stare at his purchases, but something had cropped up to prevent it. He never used the bus, enjoying the freedom his ancient car gave him.

By the time WPC Judy Robbins arrived with Sergeant Davies they were already aware that the children he had seen were neither Ronnie nor Sharon nor their friends. Blake went over it again but it was like getting blood from a stone. He was uncertain about everything: what time he went out, the time of his return, and whether he saw Mrs Black on his way out or on his return. Judy studied his grey, unemotional face and thought he looked like a man whom life has passed by. He lived alone, the dog his only companion in the isolated stone house which was shabby, untidy and none too clean. The flowerbeds were overgrown but the garden must have received some attention because the lawn was cut short. Maybe to the dog's advantage. Here and there rose bushes thrust a few sickly branches through the weeds, one or two having the strength to provide a couple of blooms, and a couple of perennials raised their heads to the sun. George Blake was sixty-nine years old but would have surprised no one had he claimed to be a decade older.

Judy raised her eyebrows when she realized they were getting nowhere. Blake was either a very vague man or was bordering on senile dementia. There were no clocks in the room into which they were shown and he did not appear to be wearing a wrist-watch. These facts went some way to explain why he was uncertain as to time. On the table were the remains of a meal. To Judy's houseproud eye it looked as if it might have been there longer than since breakfast time. Smears of egg yolk had hardened into a deeper yellow than an hour or so would allow. However, slovenliness is not a crime.

There was no further point in staying and they were not sorry to return to the blazing sunlight after the dinginess of the house.

'He struck me as lonely,' Judy commented as they got into the patrol car and drove towards their next destination. 'What was all that about, his hanging around the school?'

'Oh, years ago. I got a call from the headmistress. He wasn't doing any harm, just watching the kids playing. I spoke to him about it, you know, saying how people could misinterpret his being there, and he stopped. He was lonely enough without being thought of as a dirty old man.'

'Yet he chose to live there? There're no neighbours within shouting distance and that house is far too big for him.'

'I know, couldn't understand it when he bought it, he's got no family now. Mind you, if he is lonely, it's mostly of his own making. When he first came here a few of the women went out to see if he needed anything, more than likely to have a poke around if you ask me, but he turned them all away, said he could manage on his own. He's got his car though, and the dog – he gets out and about. The house could certainly do with some decoration, couldn't it? I don't suppose he'll bother now.'

'Has he been here long?' People's behaviour fascinated Judy. She had far more time for eccentrics, whatever shape they took, than the nine-to-five brigade with their regular meals and their mortgages.

'Difficult to remember. About six years, maybe. Wife'd be able to tell you, she always know things like that.'

'Poor old bugger.'

As they pulled into a cul-de-sac lined with modern bungalows, Judy thought of Lucy. Perhaps it was the attractive, dark-haired woman watering some pots in her front garden who sparked off the thought. She had the same build and colouring as Lucy. How had she fared with the cocky Barry Swan? She'd find out tonight. If she managed to get off duty in time they planned to go to the cinema together.

The residents in Hazel Drive and Hazel Close, which were adjoining, all displayed shock and horror at what had occurred. It had hit a couple of them badly, those who had daughters the same age and in the same class as Sharon. It was not Bob and Judy's task to speak to these children; a team of specialists from Rickenham were doing that. Sergeant Davies thought it was ridiculous and said as much.

'The police force, sorry, the police service as we have to call ourselves now, is getting like the bloody National Health Service. Go to your GP and what happens? He can't diagnose you. Maybe if there's a piece of bone sticking through your flesh he'll make a guess and say it's broken. Otherwise, what do they do? Send you to a specialist, that's what. It's an insult. I know all these folks, and their children, and they'd talk to me easier than these specialists, given the chance.' The respect Bob

Davies had developed for the city boys, as he called them, was rapidly declining. Or maybe, and he didn't like to admit it, he felt his nose had been put out of joint. He didn't like interference in what he thought of as his own personal patch. Deep down he was ashamed: such sentiments should have no place in his heart when a little girl was dead and not yet buried.

There was someone at home in each of the bungalows except one. That family were on holiday in Crete. In the other fifteen homes lived a total of seven children. Not one was playing farther away than the boundaries of their own, or a neighbour's, garden. Throughout the day, as they continued their inquiries they failed to see a child that was not accompanied. The murder had changed the friendly, easy-going structure of village life.

Almost everyone reiterated their brief statements of the previous evening, and those they had not already seen were unable to come up with anything new. The young mothers worked in town and their children spent the day with relatives or child-minders. It was the only way in which they could afford their mortgages. Then they knocked on the door of 6 Hazel Close. Celeste Palmer, wearing pink and turquoise tracksuit bottoms and a white T-shirt with matching trim, invited them in. She told them she knew why they were there. 'I heard the news this morning. It's dreadful, isn't it? We saw your van thing when we came home last night, but we never guessed it was something like this. It's really awful.' Judy and Bob had listened to all the adjectives to describe Sharon Vickers' fate but felt there wasn't a word in the English language to sum it up accurately.

'Someone did call last night, Mrs Palmer, but no one was at home.'

'Yes, Sergeant Davies.' Celeste patted her highlighted hair affectedly. 'Tony took me to the Country Club for dinner and dancing.' The Elms Golf and Country Club, which was its full title but hardly ever used, lay three miles out of Rickenham Green, but to the north of the town. Little Endesley was to the west and therefore approximately four and a half miles from the Country Club. It was an expensive venue but Tony and

70

Celeste Palmer were avid social climbers. She was not impressing Sergeant Davies, who wondered what their means of transport had been. Tony Palmer had only just got his licence back after a year's ban for drinking and driving, and he couldn't imagine the loud, brash Palmer enjoying a meal and dancing without a good few drinks under his belt. That matter could wait. More important was what Mrs Palmer was saying about yesterday afternoon.

The Palmers' two daughters had spent the night with Tony's sister in the neighbouring village of Frampton Common. In return for this favour Celeste had had her nephew and niece over for the day to give her sister-in-law a break.

'They got bored playing in the garden and started bickering, and that drives me mad. I intended to take them swimming but unfortunately Tony had the BMW. I couldn't think of anywhere to take them except the woods.' She paused. Judy and Bob did not look at each other; they knew they were supposed to be impressed yet again by the mention of Tony's car. Neither was. 'I thought the walk might tire them out. Sandra's boy's hyperactive, she has a lot to cope with. I don't like walking myself, seems pointless when you have a decent car.' Sergeant Bob Davies, most gentle of men, had a sudden vision of rubber hose-pipes. He smiled wryly to himself. That CID bloke, Markham, would have had the information out of Celeste Palmer in seconds – not that Markham was into hose-pipes, he was just one of those men who exuded menace, who terrified suspects before he opened his mouth. But Celeste Palmer was enjoying her moment of undivided attention.

'And you saw something? In the woods?'

'Oh, yes, Sergeant, I saw something all right. We were on our way back. The children had run on a bit, not out of my sight, of course, and that's when I saw him.' She closed her mouth. They would have to ask.

'Who?' Judy prompted.

'That – that creature. Jack, whatever his name is. And if you ask me, he was in a damned hurry. I'm surprised you haven't arrested him already.'

71

'What time was this, Mrs Palmer?' Bob Davies ignored her last comment.

'About quarter-past three. I didn't actually look at my watch. One doesn't, does one, unless one needs to know the time? But it can't have been much after that.'

'You're quite certain?'

'Of course I am. I'd know that foul little creature anywhere.' And then Sergeant Davies remembered that Jacko Penhaligon had once attempted to expose himself to Laura, one of Celeste's daughters, but that the child, already warned to keep away from him, had run off. But Jacko said he was in the woods at that time, and other people saw him. Carefully, Sergeant Davies wrote down what she told him.

'Thank you, Mrs Palmer.' Was she lying? As the Chief was fond of pointing out, treat everything as a lie until you can prove it otherwise. Which didn't bear thinking about. Everyone else they'd seen might also be lying.

They finished with the residents of the bungalows, left the car in the village square and started on Jasper's Alley. This was a narrow lane of six council dwellings, originally farm workers' cottages, facing the blank wall of the side of a pub. The residents were respectable and hard-working, except for the Hargreaves family. Fortunately for most of their neighbours they lived in the end house. It was only their immediate neighbours who suffered the noise. Old Man Hargreaves, when he was at home, was either drunk and shouting at the family, especially his thin, bedraggled wife, or noisily making it up with her in the front bedroom with the windows wide open for all to hear. There was not an ounce of honesty between the lot of them. It was not a generalization to say that any petty crime in the neighbourhood could be pinned on one or other of them. Their one redeeming feature was their complete loyalty to one another, for whom they would lie through their back teeth.

Judy and Bob left the Hargreaves' place mentally shaking their heads. No one knew anything. No one was saying anything. The whole lot of them claimed to have been at home on Friday afternoon watching the racing on the telly.

'Might even be true at that,' Bob said. 'They don't seem to do much else, except thieving.' Murder was a different matter; he felt it was out of their league. They were a close-knit family, the youngest child, a girl of six, adored and spoiled by all of them. Bob did not think the Hargreaves boys were involved, louts though they were.

6

It was not until Saturday evening that Detective Constable Alan Campbell was free to do anything about Harry Morgan's videos. In fact, with the murder investigation and several other things which had cropped up, he almost forgot about them. Once he felt satisfied everything else was under control he took a walk down to the large room shared by several of the CID men. The detective who were in were either typing, talking on the telephone or sitting around chatting and drinking coffee. The atmosphere was far more informal than that which prevailed in the uniformed squad, and it had taken Alan some time to get used to it.

'OK,' he said to the room in general, 'Chief's orders. Volunteers are needed.' Suddenly everyone was very busy. Alan grinned. He knew the effect his next words would produce.

'Videos.' A few heads came up. 'Porno videos. They need viewing. Loads of them.' Suddenly they were not so busy. Amazingly, they had all been about to finish for the day anyway. Things that seconds ago had appeared to be of monumental importance could wait until tomorrow.

Eventually they divided themselves into two 'shifts'. 'We can't get through them all tonight, there're too many,' Alan said.

Someone asked if they were part of the haul they were looking for.

'Child pornography? We don't know. Might be. It might also be connected with the Vickers case. Might be nothing at all. The Chief said to go through the lot.'

The first volunteers, after making any necessary calls, trooped into the projection room. They still called it that although the 16 mm projector and screen were rarely taken out of the cupboard nowadays; almost everything they dealt with was on cassette or camcorders.

Alan slotted the first video into the recording machine beneath the television and they settled back to watch.

The first two were nothing to write home about. Each lasted approximately fifty minutes and the detectives, who had seen enough in the course of their duties, and sometimes outside them, were hoping for something different. Within ten minutes or so of each they fast-forwarded them, stopping only if something grabbed their interest. They laughed and joked but they were fully aware of the seriousness of what they were doing. Had they come across child pornography it would have been another matter. There was no sign of any. The material offered no more than various adult, heterosexual couplings. Old hat.

Detective Constable Rawlings inserted the third cassette. A tall, plump, jolly-faced man in his late twenties, he looked more like an overfed sixth-former than a hard-working CID man. This was accentuated by the way he dressed. He always came to work wearing neatly pressed slacks, a white shirt and a blazer and tie. Not for him the uniform of jeans and a leather jacket.

Dutifully they watched the first few minutes. The scene shifted from a crowded room where a party was in progress, to an upstairs bedroom. And there, perfectly clearly defined, was a lovely blonde, slowly and seductively taking off her clothes.

And there the laughing and joking stopped. Alan sat rigid with disbelief. It was a mistake. A horrible trick. One of these bastards had doctored the film. The woman was naked, spread-eagled on the bed. A man hovered over her.

In one movement Alan was out of his seat and through the door. He didn't make it as far as the lavatory. He vomited on to the gleaming tiled floor and down the wall on which he was leaning. His life was over.

75

'Jesus fucking Christ!' DC Rawlings said. 'That's his wife.' Tactfully, but too late, he switched off the set.

As Moira Roper had informed her husband, the late news on Saturday night named Sharon Vickers as the victim and showed a picture of her taken by the school photographer at the end of last term. She was smiling, confidently looked straight at the camera. Ian's stomach churned; such a short time ago she'd been looking forward to moving up a class.

Detectives had interviewed Sharon's headmistress and her form teacher, who were both spending their summer holiday at home. They bore out what was already known of the girl: she was of above-average intelligence, hard-working and, although she was popular and friendly, often preferred her own company. Neither of them could imagine who would wish to harm such a delightful, happy child. They verified that there was no bullying within the school, that it was too small an establishment for such a thing to go unnoticed and, no, it was impossible that one of their children had killed her.

Ian switched off the set and went to fetch his briefcase from under the hall table. He took out a notebook. It was one in which he jotted down thoughts and ideas as they occurred to him.

Against the word 'motive' was a question mark. There was, as far as anyone could see, no motive – or rather, as he knew only too well, no apparently logical one. Under 'motive' he'd written 'porn'. So far it was the only likely explanation. If something showed up in Morgan's videos they might be on to the killer, or the man who could lead them to him. But, and this was the big but, how could an eight-year-old girl be involved and not show the slightest signs of disturbance?

He went to the bathroom and, realizing the time and knowing he wanted an early start, decided to shave then instead of in the morning. As he did so his mind kept running over all they knew. Julie Vickers seemed to be a loving, caring mother – surely she would have noticed if her daughter was upset?

Celeste Palmer. Sergeant Davies had added a few notes of his own to what she had to say. Was she simply trying to make trouble for Jacko? It would be interesting to see what the children with her had to say. Tempted as he was to ring the station and find out what progress had been made, he left it. He did not want his men to think he was constantly on their backs. And the videos? Until every single one had been seen they could not come to any conclusion. He guessed that if there was anyone spare on the night shift they would offer to help out. He smiled as he thought of Alan Campbell being in charge. He knew what a puritan he was at heart, although he tried to disguise this from his colleagues. No doubt he'd sat conscientiously in the projection room enduring the lewd remarks of the other men and hating every minute of it.

Feeling better for the shave, Ian cleaned his teeth and went to bed, very glad that tonight was the last one he had to sleep in it alone.

Lynn Morris lay in bed next to her husband. Rob was sound asleep; he no longer had a care in the world. Tonight was the first time for ages they had been out together, and they had made a real evening of it. First the six o'clock showing of a film, then a couple of drinks followed by a set price 'leave it to us' meal at the Lotus Blossom. They were unable to eat it all. They left the car at home and travelled both ways by taxi. It meant they could both relax and have a drink, and they both needed to relax. Rob was not a big drinker and after one or two failed to notice how distracted she was. He put his whole heart into this special, reconciliatory evening.

For over a year Lynn had been seeing another man. She did not blame Rob, but he candidly accepted it was mostly his fault. He was a photographer and the recession was beginning to bite. Already he'd laid off one of his men and was reduced to going out on jobs himself, preferring to keep on the dark-room boys who had more expertise in that line than himself. But it was not just that – he had become almost obsessional, to the point of taking on small jobs which his firm would not normally touch. He rushed from one venue to the next, barely taking time off to eat.

Lynn was thirty-two. She had planned to start a family in her late twenties but was glad she hadn't. They had enough money, not that Rob ever thought so, but she knew she would be stuck at home, hardly ever seeing her husband.

About a year ago she had met John. They literally bumped into each other in the street. She dropped her handbag and the contents fell on to the pavement. He offered to buy her a drink to make up for his clumsiness and it started from there. Only when John began to insist she leave Rob and go and live with him did she realize it was not what she wanted. She wanted Rob, but not the way he was.

A week previously she had cornered Rob in his office, insisting he listen to what she had to say. Shaking from head to foot she told him about John. Rob had already guessed. There were tears and apologies on both sides, Rob admitting that largely he had been using work to escape from facing the situation.

Then, on Friday, John telephoned. He wanted to see her urgently. Lynn agreed, on condition that he return the letters she had written him. They met in the woods at Little Endesley, a place where they often used to meet. She managed to keep John at arm's length although she found she was still physically attracted to him. Once the letters were safely in her bag she told him categorically she did not want to see him again. It was over. They parted sadly, but she knew she was doing the right thing.

On that Friday, when Rob had asked her where she was when he telephoned, a habit he had developed since her confession, she said she was shopping. She vowed, as she said it, that it was the last lie she would ever tell him.

On Saturday afternoon, as she was getting ready to go out, she listened to the news on the radio and spilled half a bottle of perfume when she heard Little Endesley mentioned.

Now, sleepless and guilty, she thought of what she had seen

and wondered if it had any relevance, if her silence was protecting a killer.

In the early hours she slept, appeasing her conscience with the thought that while life was over for Sharon Vickers, hers with Rob was worth saving.

At a few minutes past midnight Helen Campbell rang the station and asked to speak to her husband. Last night he had told her he'd be late, fair enough, there was a murder inquiry under way, but normally that meant nine or ten o'clock. If he was going to be later than that he always let her know. Visions of his body lying unconscious in a gutter or hospital bed floated through her mind.

'Hold on a sec, Mrs Campbell, I'll try to put you through.' Fred Whitelaw, the desk duty sergeant, was very, very glad to be able to pass the call on. It was only a matter of half an hour or so after Alan left the projection room before everyone in the building was aware of what had happened.

No one answered from the main CID room. Sergeant Whitelaw tried another extension. It was DC Rawlings who picked up the phone. Having nothing better to do with his Saturday night he had stayed on to go through more of the videos. It wasn't the same watching them on your own, and he had a good idea how he would feel if he were in Campbell's shoes. He coughed nervously; Sergeant Whitelaw had told him who was calling.

'Pete,' Helen said, 'how are you? I haven't seen you for ages.'

'Fine. No. Work, you know.'

'Is Alan there? I don't like ringing up, but he usually lets me know if he's going to be this late.'

'Ah, he's . . . No. Not at the moment.'

'Not there? You mean he's out on a job?'

Pete Rawlings had known the Campbells for several years and liked them both. He did not want to lie but he had seen Alan's face when his wife appeared on the screen. Alan was CID now, and CID men stuck together.

'Yes. Can't say what time he'll finish. Might be an all-night job.'

'Oh, I see, surveillance.'

'Yeah, sort of. I have to go now, Helen. Nice talking to you.' He replaced the receiver. It was certain to be an all-night job. Once Alan had cleaned up the passageway and then himself, one of the detectives who was just leaving had offered to give him a lift home. Alan said he wasn't going home, nor did he accept the offer of a bed at the detective's house. He did accept a lift as far as the shabby, commercial hotel down by the railway station. What he would decide to do in the morning was anybody's guess.

The weather was unbelievable. When Detective Chief Inspector Roper left his house the sky was already a deep shade of blue and not a cloud was in sight. Warmth was seeping through the pavement on the side of the road not in shadow.

There were few early-morning sounds: a milk float clattered along Belmont Terrace, unimpeded by traffic, and the few cars that passed on the main road were travelling at a respectable, Sunday morning speed. In the distance, too far away to be coming from St Luke's in the High Street, the sound of church bells carried thinly through the still air.

Ian got into his car, which he had had to park a few doors away on his return last night. The houses did not possess garages or front gardens big enough to park in and it was each man for himself when it came to a space. As it was the weekend he supposed some of his neighbours had relatives or guests staying.

He wound down the front windows and started the engine with a little smirk. How often had he grumbled when he was trying to have a lie-in about bloody fools being out and about so early on Sunday mornings?

As he neared the town centre the detritus of Saturday night became more apparent. Fried-chicken boxes, burger cartons and empty lager bottles littered the streets, some of them smashed.

As he passed a building that called itself a night-club but was no more than a disco and watering hole for under-age drinkers, he noticed dark stains on the whitewashed wall. Another stabbing or bottling? There was never a weekend without them lately. No doubt it would be neatly recorded in the incident book. Another statistic. 'Sell firewater and you're bound to get Indians', he said to himself philosophically as he waited for the traffic lights to change. It was licensed until one thirty a.m, but no one left before two. Local cab drivers both loved and loathed the place. They could charge what they liked at that time of night but they also risked not getting paid at all or their cabs or their persons being damaged. Ian turned left and swung into the police station car-park.

He was never at his best first thing in the morning. It was not quite eight o'clock as he pushed through the swing doors and felt the refreshing coolness. He had woken without the aid of his alarm, which was unusual, but he wanted to get through as much as possible before meeting Moira and the boys off the train. He had promised to collect them at Ipswich to save the tiresome journey on the branch line which, on Sundays, always seemed to have work done to it necessitating the shunting of passengers to and fro on buses. Not a pleasant way to end a holiday. Once they were settled at home and he'd listened to their news he would come back to the station.

He approached the desk, his sixth sense telling him there was trouble. There was not the normal leisurely weekend atmosphere today, and through the glass partition behind the reception desk he saw people moving around.

'Morning, sir.'

'Morning, Sarge. Busy night?'

'You could say that,' Fred Whitelaw replied, glancing at the clock. It was 8.01, his relief should be there. He pushed the incident book across the counter, turning it so the writing faced the Chief.

'Bloody hell.'

'That's one way of putting it, sir,' Whitelaw said sardonically. 'I shan't be sorry to get home to my bed.' He looked pointedly at the large clock with its clear, Arabic numbers which they'd salvaged from the old place. Still no sign of Jones. OK, the man's wife had just had a baby and no doubt it cried all night, but every minute after clocking-off time seemed like an hour.

Ian walked up to his office. What had got into people last night? There was no full moon, which often accounted for a rise in crime. Maybe it was the heat. The night had been muggy and humid and even with the windows thrown wide open, Ian had had difficulty sleeping. He'd pushed all the bedclothes to the floor but could not bring himself, like Moira, to sleep naked. He had tried it once or twice but found he felt extremely vulnerable.

He tried to recall the crimes: two stabbings, neither fatal, eight reported burglaries, a fatal road traffic accident in which two people died, a suspected case of arson in which all the stock of a closing-down sale was destroyed and in which the building blazed so fiercely that part of the one-way system had to be closed for a couple of hours. Insurance investigators were working on it now. What else? Numerous driving and taking-aways, including one joyrider who collided with a parked car and was rewarded for his efforts with a broken nose when he hit the windscreen – and serve him damn well right, Ian thought uncharitably. Complaints of noisy parties and barking dogs.

And Jacko Penhaligon in the cells.

This piece of information was only just sinking into his early-morning brain when there was a knock at his door. DC Rawlings' plump face appeared before the rest of his equally plump body.

'Sorry to bother you so early, sir. I was told you were in. I wanted to give you this myself.' Rawlings had also made an effort to rise early. He'd gone straight home, there being nowhere but the dreaded discos to get a drink last night, and consequently, not having a Sunday morning hangover, had not found it too difficult. And Alan Campbell was a mate. He handed the Chief a typed, signed report. 'I wanted to let you know myself.'

'Thank you, Ro . . . Rawlings. Does it need looking at right away?' He stopped himself in time from calling him Roly, the name by which he was familiarly known.

'I think so, sir.'

When Pete Rawlings had left his office Ian read the report. He was horrified. Of all the men under him Alan Campbell was the last one it should have happened to, the one he thought least able to cope with it. He must talk to him as soon as possible. Rawlings had done right in making a report; it would be put in his personnel file. Such things could adversely affect a man's career, could turn him into a woman-hater or worse. He might not be so unbiased when it came to dealing with domestic disputes or prostitution or even female colleagues. As soon as he came in he'd have a word.

Ian heard his stomach rumbling. He hadn't bothered to make tea before he left so he decided to go down to the canteen and remedy the situation; then he wanted to see what Jacko had been up to. Was the Sharon Vickers case solved? No, of course not. Someone would have rung him at home. He had not looked to see what he was charged with – there was too much else in the incident book to take it all in. A cup of tea and maybe his brain would start functioning. And a piece of toast, thick with butter and to hell with the consequences.

When it arrived the toast was brown and thin-sliced and didn't taste anywhere near as good as the doorsteps Flo put under the grill at the old place, whose outsides were crisp and whose insides were warm and doughy. He carried his tray to an empty table but on the way spotted Pat Livingstone sitting at a table on her own. For no particular reason he decided to join her.

'May I?' he asked, indicating the chair opposite her.

Her face lit up. 'Yes, of course.'

'Weekend on?'

'Yes. I'm waiting for Sergeant Barker, but I was a bit early. I know Little Endesley isn't very big, but we're still on the door-to-door. Mostly farms outside the village now.'

'I see.' Ian was thoughtful. The children's statements would be to hand by now and no doubt a lot of things didn't tie up.

83

He bit into his toast and washed it down with a sip of tea. He noticed Pat Livingstone had washed her hair; she had, in fact, got up early to do so, and she was also wearing make-up. Unfortunately it did nothing to improve her complexion. Either her mirror was badly situated or she was unskilled in applying the stuff because whatever was on her face had a caked appearance and highlighted rather than concealed her acne scars. Ian felt a pang of sympathy for the young woman and smiled broadly by way of compensation. He did not know that she would carry the memory of that smile around with her for ages, that the hairwashing and make-up were for his benefit.

What he did know was that if the investigation was still on then Jacko was not the culprit. He had better find out what he was doing in the cells.

Bolting the last of the toast and finishing his tea he stood up and excused himself. Pat Livingstone watched him leave with a wistful expression in her eyes.

It didn't take long to discover what Jacko had been up to, and Ian found it hard not to take his side.

He listened patiently while Jacko told his story.

Once the gatepost was repaired he went home. Expecting Janet and the boys to return soon he made a pot of tea and smoked a couple of roll-ups. They were late. As the minutes ticked by he felt the cold, clutching fingers of panic. He told himself the bus was late or had broken down. He made more tea, laughing at his own stupidity; she'd missed it, that was all, they'd be on the next one. At five o'clock he knew they weren't coming back.

It was then he poured himself a glass of home-made cider hoping it would quell the rising fury. 'Bastards!' he shouted to the four walls. 'Police bastards! Why can't they leave us alone?' After a second glass of cider bravado took over from sense. He took the Land Rover which belonged to Gerald Langdon, and drove into Rickenham, taking care because he did not want to damage his employer's possession. He parked it in a pay-and-display place and locked it before entering the nearest pub. He was going to the station to tell them exactly what he thought.

But not just yet. When a man's wife and kids left him he was entitled to a little drink. He rarely used the pubs in town and saw no one he knew. It was getting on for closing time before he felt he had the right words to convey to the police what he thought of them.

Staggering down the High Street he bumped into people. A few were annoyed, but mostly they tittered at his erratic progress. His entry to the police station was not the most dignified. Befuddled by drink he stumbled as the swing door started revolving before he was quite ready, and it expelled him in a heap on the floor of the reception area. Picking himself up he yelled, 'Swan!' Fred Whitelaw, whose back was turned at the time, was startled.

'Get that bastard Swan down here. And Roper. I'll teach them to interfere.'

'Can I help you, sir?' Whitelaw's face was impassive, not a muscle twitched. He'd seen it all before.

'Yesh, you bloody well can. I wanna see Swan.'

'Detective Sergeant Swan is not on the premises at the moment. Can anyone else – '

'Swan!' Jacko bellowed, even louder. 'Get your arse down here. I know you're up there.'

The noise was heard half-way round the building and several men came into the reception area. Jacko put up a good fight. That is, he thought he did. He struggled as hard as he was able but the couple of swings he took missed their mark by some way. He was booked on a drunk and disorderly. One of the men knew him and said he was harmless enough, not to bother with attempted assault on the police officer. He spent the night in the cells, for the first couple of hours incurring the wrath of the others held there who were trying to get some sleep. Eventually he quietened down and slept off his excesses.

Ian could picture it clearly. It was almost comical, except that if Janet Penhaligon had left him he didn't like to think what would become of Jacko.

However, hungover, wifeless, and locked in a cell, he might be prepared to say where he really was on Friday afternoon.

Jacko's face was greenish-grey. He was not used to so much drink – he rarely drank, he had no one to do so with. He recalled little of the events of the previous evening but when he saw Roper and not a lesser individual he began to think the worst.

'I know I was shouting, I wanted to see Swan, but after that I don't know what happened. I haven't hurt no one, have I?'

Ian shok his head. 'OK, Jacko. You say Janet's left you. Could this be because of something she knows? Something that happened on Friday afternoon?'

'No. I swear to God, I never done it. It's true, last night I could've done murder, but no kid. Not me.'

Ian believed him. 'Someone'll be down to take a statement, not that I suppose it'll do much good, then you'll be free to go.'

'What'll they do to me?'

'A fine. Nothing more.'

Jacko accepted his fate with a long face, and Ian left him to it.

On his desk was the information gleaned from the children of Little Endesley. Ian read what Ronnie Vickers had to say first, but it told him little more than what Julia Vickers said. Ronnie had still been in shock when he was seen on Saturday morning, but it couldn't wait, those early hours are the most important, when memories are still fresh, when wished-for events are not confused with fact. Sharon had initially gone with Ronnie and his friends, but had then, as she often did, decided to go off on her own. He did not see her after about quarter-past two. By gently probing, the officer trained in dealing with children discovered that the fear Ronnie was displaying was because he thought his parents would blame him. The officer knew it would take a good deal of patience and reassurance to get that idea out of the boy's head. He hoped the parents were up to it. 'She said', Ronnie told him, 'she was going to try to find Michael.'

'Oh no,' Ian said aloud to himself, 'it can't be.' Was this the reason Janet left? Not to get away from her husband but to protect her son? Michael had not yet been interviewed. He was not at home on Saturday morning or later when they called back.

The Chief skimmed through the rest of the reports. Michael Penhaligon must be found.

Jacko signed a statement which he hardly bothered to read, then he was given back his possessions. It was nearly ten before he was released. He left the station and walked out into the blinding sunlight, his head thumping, his eyes screwed up against the glare. His reflexes and concentration were at such odds that he was almost knocked down as he crossed the street. The driver of the approaching car blasted his horn; the sound left Jacko trembling and sweating. He headed up the High Street, trying to remember where he'd left the Land Rover – he knew it would be somewhere safe. He read the sign in the car-park: there was no charge on Sundays.

He wondered if he was up to driving but there was nowhere open in Rickenham where he could get a cup of coffee. He had drunk half a cup in his cell but it was foul. He turned the ignition key, his head pounding anew with the noise and vibration. Slowly and carefully he made his way home.

He parked under the shade of some trees and walked towards the cottage. He knew he had had two glasses of cider before he left last night, but he was nowhere near drunk then, certainly not drunk enough to leave the front door wide open. He approached it, shaking. Janet must have come back.

There was no time to ponder over the statements of small children or the misdeamenours of Jacko Penhaligon. The Chief was hardly back in his office before there was another knock at his door. His initial suspicions when he had arrived were proving correct. This was no peaceful Sunday morning.

'Come in.'

DC Alan Campbell stood before him, looking almost as bad as Jacko had.

'Good morning, Alan.' The Chief indicated the chair in front of his desk.

Alan ignored it and, instead, placed his identity card on the deck.

'I shan't be needing this any more, sir. I want to resign.'

Interesting way of putting it, the Chief thought. Not, I have resigned, but, I want to resign. Which, in his book, meant the opposite.

'My letter of resignation's in there.' He placed an envelope on the desk. 'And my reasons. It's nothing personal, I mean nothing to do with anyone here.' Because his reasons were definitely personal.

'Would you like to tell me about it?'

'No, sir. I've had all night to think about it and I can't stay. You'll understand why when you read the letter.' It had not occurred to Alan that, apart from the men who were with him last night, almost everyone else was also aware of his problems; had he witnessed the same thing happening to someone else, he would have kept his mouth shut. But most people were not like Alan Campbell and he would have been mortified beyond belief had he known it was common knowledge.

'I can't accept it.' Alan was not prepared for this. 'I cannot let one of my best men go without at least having the opportunity to discuss the reasons. I think I've been fair with you and therefore the least you can do is give me an explanation. And if it doesn't concern anyone here at the station, I fail to see why you have to leave. I know, I know,' he continued, holding up a hand to silence Alan's protestations, 'it's all in the letter. You are, however, doing me a great disservice if you feel you can't trust me enough to discuss the problem.' The Chief watched his expression. He saw that Alan badly wanted to get it off his chest, but that his pride prevented him. 'Look, son,' he said gently, 'have a seat and tell me about it.'

The tears which Alan had not shed the night before burned behind his eyelids and fell, unexpectedly, in a hot stream down his face, blurring his vision. He did not have time to turn away.

'I'm sorry,' he mumbled, 'I'm sorry.' He sat down. The long

night without sleep had left him weak and vulnerable, exhausted by recurring pictures of Helen performing those acts with other men. The Chief, who had witnessed the effects of personal tragedy, on his men as well as outsiders, many times throughout his career, said nothing. He waited until Alan had his emotions under control, knowing he would talk then.

At last it all came out. How he believed Helen was modelling underwear, how he never questioned the extra money she earned and how flattered and happy it made him feel when she spent that money on him. 'Conscience gifts, that's all they were,' he said.

The Chief knew, without doubt, that whatever Helen Campbell was involved in, her husband had no part in it. That was something. Too many times lately members of the force had been put on the line; he didn't want it to happen in his division.

'I can't pretend to know what you're going through, no one can, but I *can* guess. There are several ways to look at it, and I'm not talking about your personal life – how you sort that out is your own affair. Unfortunately, we'll have to speak to her ourselves, but – '

'No. I never want to set eyes on her again.'

'Let me finish, Alan. You'll have to at some point, whatever decision you make. However, we're smack in the middle of a murder inquiry, one in which you are playing an invaluable part. If you leave, someone else'll have to pick up the pieces, and that someone may not be as well organized and precise as you, and whoever it is will have to be pulled off another job. You said you feel that your life is over – that feeling will pass. But the same cannot be said for Sharon Vickers, her short life is definitely over. I could offer you sick leave but I don't think there's much to be gained from that, it'll only give you time to brood and we'd still be a man short. My suggestion is, and I think it's the best way, that instead of running away, you face the people who know. In our game it's a small world – coppers move around, wherever you go, whatever you do, there's always the chance someone will find out and you have to face the same thing over again. The sooner you get it over with, the better, and you'll be amongst men and women who care about you.' The Chief hoped he wasn't overdoing it. 'What I'm saying is, stay, at least until this case is wrapped up. If you feel the same later, then by all means apply for a transfer or whatever. And besides,' he added, knowing he'd played the heavy long enough, 'who's going to talk football with me if you go?'

Alan stared at his clasped hands, the knuckles were white, but there was the vaguest hint of a smile around the corners of his mouth when he heard the last words. Only a hint, but it was there.

'OK, sir, I'll stay until the end of the case and take it from there.' He stood up, aware that he'd taken up enough of the Chief's time.

'Alan?' He looked around. 'Haven't you forgotten something?'

This time he did smile as he took the envelope and his card from the desk and stuffed them into the hip pocket of his jeans.

'Go on, son, get downstairs and have a shower and some breakfast then have a go at these.' He put the statements taken from the children of Little Endesley into a large brown envelope and handed them to him.

Alan nodded; he felt better already. The Chief had a way of getting straight to the heart of the matter, picking out the important things. He loved being in the CID and he loved working at Rickenham Green. The Chief had made it possible for him to stay without losing face. Later he would decide what to do about Helen; for the moment he was going to concentrate on the job in hand.

The Chief sighed, then groaned when he saw how late it was. He must leave immediately if he was to be on time to meet the train.

He concentrated only on his driving until he was on the A12. It was relatively free of traffic and he was able to let his mind wander. When he had more than one problem he dealt with them by making mental lists. Number one priority was finding the killer of Sharon Vickers and he didn't want the operation

90

screwed up by one unstable DC, whose mind was on his wife rather than his job. His gut feeling was that the man would pull through, but he would keep a discreet eye on him.

What puzzled him most was the seeming lack of motive. If Michael Penhaligon was the culprit, anything could be going on in his head. He might not have the mental age of a seventeen-year-old but he was by no means stupid. Supposing he'd overheard his parents rowing over Sharon and decided to remove the cause of the arguments? Maybe. But there were no facts, nothing to substantiate this. And still in the back of his mind lay that other dreadful maybe. The one that said it was a total stranger, someone passing through. The case might stay on the books, unsolved, for ever. He, and everyone he worked with, dreaded that more than anything else.

He arrived at Ipswich station with no time to spare and had to run to be on the platform as the train pulled in. It didn't help matters, he was hot and sweaty already from the drive. There, at last, after a week that seemed like a month, was Moira. She was, and could only ever be, the one woman for him.

He had married her straight from college, a little perturbed about the fifteen-year age gap, but Moira reassured him it didn't matter. She had always assumed she would marry a man who was older, more mature, than herself. She was not what in those days was called a 'raver'; she disliked crowds and parties, and she knew, even if her husband didn't, that he would not be preventing her from enjoying her youth – her enjoyment came from quieter pursuits. She had always seemed content to be his wife and Mark's mother until the bombshell of a few months ago when she said she was going back to college to take a secretarial course. He smiled as he remembered the row there'd been, and her naïvety in buying a book on shorthand, quite forgetting she would learn the skills needed to operate modern technology. Of course, this gave her more to talk to Mark about as he was computer-mad.

'Ian?' She stood on tiptoe to kiss him and was pleasantly surprised when he grabbed her round the waist and gave her a lingering kiss full on the mouth. When he released her, Mark and his friend, Danny, were busily looking at anything other than two adults making fools of themselves in public.

Ian ruffled Mark's head, remembering too late how much he hated it, how it disturbed the carefully gelled hair which remained in place even in a high wind. He did know better than to kiss him. 'Missed you, son.'

'Mm,' Mark said, followed by something Ian couldn't make out but which he hoped expressed the same sentiments.

Moira looked great. Her light brown hair was streaked blonde where the sun and the salt had bleached it, her skin was tanned a golden brown. The cool cotton dress she wore flattered her figure, which she kept in shape by diet. Beside her Ian felt untidy and in need of a bath. Mark looked well, too. Gone were the dark circles from under his eyes which had appeared during the end-of-term exams. His face was aglow with health. He started chatting about boat trips and fishing and Gran's peculiar habits, both boys laughing at certain words which had become private jokes between them.

Ian loaded their luggage into the boot. They travelled light. The boys' requirements were packed in flight bags and Moira's in a small suitcase. In her hand was a carrier bag which she kept with her.

They dropped Danny off at his house and Moira got out to have a few words with his mother, reassuring her he'd been no trouble, then they headed towards Belmont Terrace. Inside, Moira handed him the carrier. 'For you. A present.' He looked inside the bag. It contained two pastel-coloured short-sleeved shirts, a reward for his dieting, she told him. He wondered if he was too old for such finery, and also if he'd put on weight in her absence. He thanked her and promised to try them on later.

Moira disappeared into the garden. She was astonished at how quickly things had grown in the time she was away. Ian must have taken some notice of the list she had left: the tubs and flowerbeds had been watered. It was not until several days later when she was chatting to her neighbour that she learned he'd taken pity on the wilting plants and shot jets of water over the fence from his own hose-pipe.

Mark also disappeared immediately, making Ian feel almost redundant. Within minutes what he called music was thumping its bass notes down through the ceiling. Ian shook his head. He'd be glad to get back to work.

'You look tired, love. Fancy a coffee?' Moira asked, having satisfied herself the garden was all right.

'Yes, but it'll have to be quick.' He didn't look at her, he couldn't bear to see her face drop. She had only been home a matter of minutes and he was about to rush off.

She rested a hand on his arm. 'I know. I hadn't forgotten. Are you getting anywhere?'

'No, absolutely nowhere. Not a damn lead at all. Anyway, you don't want to hear about the job the second you walk through the door. I forgot to tell you, you look terrific – and I'm pleased you both had a good time.'

'We did, but I was so glad Danny came along. Mark would've been bored stiff if he'd only had mum and me for company. Look, get a coffee at work, I can see you're itching to get back.'

Was it that obvious? 'I'll just tell Mark I'm off.' After the traumas of the previous year he was not going to ignore his son: no more going out without saying goodbye, no more broken promises. He was learning to treat him like a human being even if, at times, he didn't behave like one. He had to knock loudly to make himself heard. Mark knew what was coming, mum had warned him, but at least the old man recognized he existed.

'Hope you catch him soon,' Mark said before he turned up the volume on his tape deck again.

After that brief interlude with his family Ian returned to the station. Just knowing Moira would be there when he got home was enough to ease some of the tension.

Which was a very good thing because, pacing his office like a caged tiger, Superintendent Ross awaited him.

*

93

Jacko approached his front door with caution. He didn't want to startle Janet. On the other hand, was it her who was in there? Word could have got around that he'd been banged up for the night, and someone might have taken the opportunity to break in. He was not in a fit state to tangle with an intruder. He poked his head round the door.

'Well, there you are then,' Dorothy Davies said, smoothing down her dress. 'What a to-do.' Jacko, his hangover raging and showing no signs of abatement, was even more confused. He had no idea what the woman was talking about or what she was doing in his house. 'The boys were worried when you weren't here.'

'The boys?' If they were home, Janet must be, but where was she? It was all too much. He stumped into the kitchen and sank into his sagging armchair next to the range, allowing Dorothy to put the kettle on while she explained the misunderstanding.

'Janet was taken ill,' she told him, hastily pushing him back into the chair. 'Now calm down, let me tell you. She's all right now, but she had a bit of a turn in Fine Fare, fainted and hit her head on the edge of the check-out desk. They sensibly called an ambulance which took her over to Rickenham General for X-rays. The boys had to go too as there was no one to watch out for them. You'd've been proud of little Brian, he told the ambulanceman that they couldn't go home on the bus together because although his brother was big he'd been to a special school and they were supposed to have a grown-up with them. And you know what hospitals are like,' she continued, well into her stride now, 'they keep you hanging around for ages. By the time your poor wife was seen in Casualty and the X-rays done, time was getting on, and she had to wait for a bed because they wanted to keep her in overnight for observation. They always do, you know, with head injuries. And then the boys didn't know anyone's phone number, and with you not having a phone yourself it was a bit awkward. It wasn't until about seven that Janet was in a fit state to tell them what to do. She asked them to ring us at the police house.' Jacko decided there and then that he would ask Gerald Langdon to install a telephone, which he'd offered to do on numerous occasions. Jacko had refused, because he didn't like the things, it wasn't natural to talk into a piece of plastic, and he was shy and ill at ease with the instrument. But if it saved another night like last night he'd put up with it.

'Did the boys stay at the hospital?'

'Oh no, they've nowhere to put them. When the ward sister rang I went over to fetch them. Bob's busy at the moment with . . . well, you know, and when we came back you weren't here so I decided to keep them overnight. Bob popped up about ten thirty to let you know but there was still no sign of you. He thought you were either out working or had heard and gone to the hospital so he put a note through the door. Here it is.' She handed it to him. 'It was still there when we came this morning.' Dorothy did not quote her husband's actual words, which were, 'I hope the bleeder hasn't gone and done a runner;' she was far too tactful. 'Janet gave me the key, in case the boys needed anything. They've gone out to play – I'll give them a shout.'

There was no need. They had heard the familiar sound of the Land Rover in the distance and come running back. They burst in through the kitchen door. 'Dad!' Brian said excitedly. 'We've been to the new hospital and then we stayed with Mrs Davies and she gave us – '

'All right, Brian, dear. I think your dad needs a bit of peace and quiet.' Jacko blushed, knowing she had made a shrewd guess as to the events of the previous night. Once the boys had gone outside again he told her what had happened, knowing it would go no further than her husband.

Sergeant Davies had not informed Rickenham that Jacko was missing. He liked to deal with things at a steady pace. For a start it wasn't certain Jacko was missing – he really might have gone to the hospital or be out in the woods. More than likely, when Janet didn't return he'd gone looking for her. Sergeant Davies knew he would not be able to exist without her. If he had bunked off he would soon be picked up. He had no money and nowhere to go and he would never survive in a town.

'Tell you what,' Dorothy said, 'why don't I mind the boys

95

while you go into Rickenham? They're no trouble, and they can have a bit of dinner with me. They said Janet could come home this morning if everything was all right.'

'It's very kind of you, ma'am, and last night. Thanks.' Jacko was genuinely grateful; there had been few times in his life when anyone, apart from his wife, had done him a kindness. 'I'd best get along then. Will she want anything?'

'No, she's got all her clothes.'

Jacko nodded, wishing he could find the words to express what he felt. Dorothy patted his arm. She knew, she could see it in his eyes.

The Chief stifled a groan. If Ross was in his office at any time it meant trouble. But on a Sunday? Ross wanted results. He always wanted results, but acted as though he had the monopoly on this particular desire. He seemed unable to comprehend that the men under him also worked towards the same end, albeit for various reasons. For some it was pride in their job, for others another notch in their belt, for men like Barry Swan it was another step towards promotion. They all felt that criminals should not be allowed to go free, pursuing whichever vileness provided their livelihood. Black and white, as simple as that. And the best, the men like Ian Roper, combined all those views but diluted them with compassion and the desire to keep the streets safe for decent people. Not so Superintendent Ross. He only wanted results, and he wanted them yesterday.

Doc Harris had not been able to persuade Ross on to the greens of the Country Club of which they were both members. The Doc, it was known, took a drink or two, and he more than made up for his annual subscription by drinking there: they only charged £1.30 for doubles of whisky and gin, and the Doc drank whisky. Marcus Ross sipped an occasional scotch, but always with loads of ice and a large splash of soda. He took his golf seriously, played well and, with the exception of the Doc, with the right people. He was cultivating rumours whose dubious origins rumbled from much higher up that he was in line for a knighthood. He'd done everything possible, donating large amounts of his inherited personal wealth to charities, patronizing causes and cultivating the right people. Sir Marcus Ross. It sounded good, had the right ring to it. But those who knew him, knew better. For one thing his wife had left him and he was not important enough except in his own eyes. Out of his hearing words like pompous ass, prig and social climber were bandied about.

Ross was fifty-five and had risen quickly and effortlessly up through the ranks, constantly denying nepotism despite having a Chief Constable as an uncle and his ex-father-in-law at the Yard. When his wife had walked out five years previously, taking with her all her jewellery and as many of the family heirlooms as she could cram into the back of her car, she had left him a note which was brief, but to the point. 'Marcus,' she wrote, 'you have bored me rigid for twenty-five years. Good-bye.' Even this he did not take as a personal affront but put it down to his wife being shallow and ungrateful.

The Chief always reminded himself of this whenever he faced Ross; that way he became easier to deal with. The note became public knowledge because Ross's cleaning lady found it propped against a rose bowl on the dining-room table and it was too good a bit of gossip to keep to herself.

'What progress has been made on the Vickers case, Roper?' No good afternoon, no pleasantries or comments about the unbearable heat, just the direct question. 'How are your men doing?' Typical. They were Roper's men until the case was solved, then they would become Ross's men.

'We're still at the fact-gathering stage, sir. The problem seems to be lack of motive.'

'I see. No progress at all. Get me the files.'

Ian clenched his teeth. 'Please,' he muttered under his breath, hating the fact that, despite all the jokes, Ross was still his boss. For all his pride in his work Ross always made him feel like a stupid office junior. He unlocked his drawer and took out the the most relevant file. Ross took it from him and sat down behind Ian's desk. He turned the pages slowly and deliberately as if the typewritten words were pages of a priceless manuscript. Next to Moira's cool, fresh prettiness Ian had felt grubby. Compared with Ross, who was immaculately turned out, he felt like a tramp.

'Hmm.' Non-committal though this was, it pleased Ian no end; it said everything. Ross had found nothing with which to pick fault. 'You seem to have it under control.'

'Yes, sir.'

'Rather baffling, this lack of motive?'

'Yes, sir.' Two could play at being non-committal.

'Well, keep me informed, Roper. Mustn't detain you.'

'Yes, sir.'

Then he was gone. 'What on earth was all that about?' Ian asked himself; he'd been expecting a roasting at the very least.

'Oh, by the way . . .' Ian turned around. Here it comes, he thought, as Ross reappeared. 'The pornography angle. Anything there?'

'Not yet, sir, so far it's just the usual. At least what we have in our possession is – we're following it up, of course.'

'Yes. Good. Goodbye.'

Ian waited to make sure he really had gone before taking his own seat. On the right side of the desk a sense of his place in the scheme of things gradually returned. Still thinking about Ross's visit he jumped and almost knocked the telephone off the desk when it rang.

'Don't know what it means, sir,' DC Campbell told him, 'but I thought you'd want to know. Celeste Palmer claims she saw Jacko on Friday afternoon in the woods, but her children, and her sister's children, said they didn't go into the woods, only walked alongside of them, and although they mentioned one or two people, they didn't see Jacko. They know who he is, they've been warned to keep away from him. And Sergeant Davies reports that he tried it on with Laura Palmer several years ago.'

'So Mrs Palmer has an axe to grind.'

'Exactly, sir.'

'Well done, Campbell. And thanks. I'll get someone over to see her.'

The Chief rang the incident room at Little Endesley and said he wanted someone to see Mrs Palmer again, and why.

It took next to no time to ascertain that Celeste Palmer had lied. She blushed and backtracked furiously, trying to convince her interviewers that dear Sergeant Davies, whom she had known for years, must have misunderstood her. She was informed that she might be charged with wasting police time and was left alone with her family and her conscience. She burst into tears. 'I hate him, that filthy little bastard. What does it matter if he did it or not? He should've been locked up years ago.' She was not the only one in the village to think that way. Tony poured her a large glass of the dry white wine which they'd been enjoying in the back garden before the interruption, and told her not to worry.

'No sense of humour, those flatfoots,' he said. 'Look what they did to me.'

Tony, because of his drink/driving case, did not have a high opinion of the police. He was the type of man who readily placed blame anywhere except on his own shoulders. The police had arrested him, therefore it was their fault he had been banned; it was ridiculous – he could hold his drink. Jacko – now, that was one area where he and his wife were in complete agreement. *His* daughter had been involved; anyone else's and it might have been more understandable, but not when it was his little Laura. And what had happened? Damn all, that's what. Just a severe warning for Jacko and the police saying he hadn't actually done anything and that Laura had had the good sense to run. Now they had the effrontery to disturb his family on a Sunday afternoon and accuse his wife of lying – and worse, threaten to charge her. Who did they think they were dealing with? They were not riff-raff like some in the village, the Hargreaves lot, for instance. A man in his position should be treated with respect. Well, perhaps it was time to show them, time to take matters into his own hands. He poured another large glass of wine and, seeing the bottle was empty, gave it to

Celeste and went back into the house for the gin. He took it outside and sat down to ponder over how he would show them who was boss.

On Sunday night Dorothy Davies called for Mrs Black and together they walked down to the village hall for their weekly session of bingo. It was a bit of a shambles; all the boxes containing things for the fête had to be pushed to one side and the folding tables and chairs, which were also used for the whist drive, taken out and put up. The chance of winning up to fifteen pounds was too much to deter most of the regulars.

'You look a bit better this evening, dear,' Dorothy said to her companion. 'But what a lot's going on! What with poor little Sharon and the Penhaligons . . .'

'Was it him then, after all?'

'Oh, no. Janet took a turn for the worse in Fine Fare and had to be taken to Rickenham General. I had the boys last night. Good as gold they were, too. I'll say that for Jacko, whatever else he's done, he knows how to bring up his own kids. Very polite they were, and offered to help with the dishes. It must've happened just after I saw you.'

'In the butcher's? Yes. Old Man Blake was there too. I knew it couldn't be true, that he only lives off the tinned stuff the post office delivers to him. Mind you, Mrs Harper saw his order being put up and she said there were half a dozen tins of everything. You will help me out, won't you, if I can't concentrate?'

Dorothy understood the shock Mrs Black had suffered and in her position would also have found it hard to concentrate on the ten bingo cards she inevitably bought. 'Of course I will. Did you sleep any better last night?'

'I did. Doctor gave me some pills. I don't think I'll ever forget, ever forget . . .' Mrs Black couldn't continue, she was weeping into her handkerchief. Dorothy put her arm around her and offered to take her home.

100

'No. I've got to start getting over it some time. Come on, take no notice of me, I'm a foolish old woman.'

Dorothy thought otherwise. Considering her age and her health, she was being remarkably brave.

Sunday night and the case was no further forward. They were running out of avenues to explore and even Ross had not been able to find fault. It was beginning to feel like a dead-end investigation. The initial burst of adrenalin was subsiding, the enthusiasm waning. Forty-eight hours and already ennui was setting in. It always did eventually, but not usually this quickly, not usually until several false leads had been followed and suspects interrogated and released. They had no leads and no real suspects. There was Morgan, maybe. Blake, for the simple reason he'd once hung around the village school. And Jacko – and the Chief knew there was more than one officer who would be only too happy to pin it on him.

The Chief decided to make one last call then go home. He read what WPC Robbins and Sergeant Davies had to say about Blake, which amounted to very little, but he had been in the woods.

Blake opened his front door as far as the length of chain would allow and looked out through the crack suspiciously with one eye. 'Detective Chief Inspector Roper,' Ian said, showing his identity. 'A few minutes of your time, if you don't mind?' It was a demand more than a request. Blake let him in and showed him into the same room where Judy and Bob Davies had stood the previous day.

'I'd just like you to tell me one more time about your movements on Friday afternoon, Mr Blake.'

'I know why you're doing this, I know what they say about me in the village. It's because I live on my own and don't join in their stupid little activities. And that business a few years back. I couldn't believe it. I know village life is parochial, but to have the police asking me to keep away from the school. Did

101

they think I was hoping for a glimpse of the girls' knickers or something? It makes me sick. They wouldn't understand. There was one girl, you see, reminded me of my own daughter. She died.' He stopped for a second or two as if he was about to say something then changed his mind. 'Just for a minute or two I could believe she was still alive. I wasn't doing any harm.'

'I'm sure no one holds that against you, sir. Now, Friday afternoon.'

'I've told two lots of your people already. I can't recall exact times, there's no reason why I should, I wasn't doing anything other than taking Beth for a walk.' At the sound of her name the collie looked up from where she was lying in her basket. 'I saw a couple of children but I don't know who they were, I hardly know anyone's name. And Mrs Black. There you are, why don't you ask her what time it was? I often see her, she seems like a sensible woman. She says hello politely and leaves it at that, she doesn't try to come round here poking her nose into my business. There's nothing else I can tell you. Goodnight, Inspector.'

Ian left. It seemed Bob Davies was right. The man obviously enjoyed his own company and that of his dog and was quite happy in his own way. There were thousands of old men who chose to live the same way. Mildly eccentric, he thought, as he started the car.

Detective Sergeant Barry Swan, convinced he was no ordinary copper but one who deserved the next promotion going, stayed on at the station, using the room DC Alan Campbell had vacated an hour earlier when he became too tired to concentrate. He took out all the files and went through them again. There were numerous people in and around the woods between the relevant times. One of them had to have seen something. Campbell might have missed it.

He thought hard. The simple, and obviously true, explanation was that someone was lying. Someone, somewhere had seen something and either was not admitting it or claimed not to

102

have been there in the first place. But who? Little Endesley was a very small place, so small that the lie might not have been deliberate. It could well be that one person forgot seeing another because they were used to their paths meeting on a daily basis. Maybes were no good – he had heard that often enough from the Chief. Facts, and facts alone, were what counted.

Every one of the videos had now been viewed but they held no clue to Sharon's murder. They contained nothing nasty, nothing disgusting – depending, of course, on one's definition of the words – but certainly nothing involving children. But if the wife of one of their men was earning a bob or two on the side in that manner, then surely their source had to be local. And that source might be producing and selling other less harmful material. Barry decided it was time to pay Mrs Alan Campbell a visit and only briefly wondered why no one else had done so yet. The Chief could have told him. It was because he wanted to give Campbell a chance to speak to his wife before he set his men loose on her.

Alan, an hour before Barry's arrival in his room, had realized his efforts were worse than useless through lack of sleep and had decided to go and get some rest. Helen rang twice during the course of the day but he refused to take her calls. Once again, it was DC Rawlings who covered for him the first time, not actually saying, but managing to imply, that Alan was still out on a job. On the second occasion the desk sergeant was truthfully able to say he was out. Alan had left a message with him to say he was going to take a walk to clear his head. Her requests to ring back were ignored because he had no idea what to say to Helen. Whatever it was, it could not be done over a telephone.

He returned to his hotel by the railway station, got his key and went up to his room. He lay on the bed, exhausted, certain he would fall asleep immediately. It was not to be. He found himself wide awake again, unable to rid his mind of pictures of Helen. There was nothing for it but to go to the bar. A couple of drinks and maybe he'd know how to approach the problem, or at least they might knock him out for an hour or so. Helen could sweat it out a bit longer; it was nothing compared to what she'd put him through. He wondered if she knew yet that he'd found out. If so, she would not be able to face another day without confronting him, offering her excuses. He'd lived with her long enough to know that much. Perhaps he should see her right away, before she caused any further embarrassment by turning up at the station and making a scene.

Downstairs in the bar he ordered a whisky from the overweight landlady. She looked at him through narrowed eyes, her experience telling her this was no travelling salesman, this was a man with troubles. His face, as he took the first sip, confirmed as much. Hardened whisky drinkers did not wrinkle their noses at the taste. Well, she was there if he wanted to talk, otherwise she'd say nothing.

Barry assumed Campbell had gone to his own house. He looked at his watch. Nine p.m. No time like the present. They'd probably made it up by now and it would be better all round if Alan was there when she was interviewed, it would get everything out in the open. However, he couldn't go alone and he needed a female with him.

Oh boy, was he out of luck. The only one available was Judy Robbins. He had to admit that, although she disliked him, she did her job conscientiously and didn't stoop to putting him down in public. She often worked late when she was between boyfriends, and she was often between them. She knew men found her too aggressive but refused to change her ways. Her mother had died when she was three and she had been brought up by her father to be independent and strong. If men didn't like her the way she was, too bad. She was not going to become the doting little woman content to take second place.

'Judy? Would you do me a favour?' Barry was very polite. 'Would you mind coming to see Mrs Campbell with me?' He could have insisted, she was still on duty, but he didn't want to get off to a bad start, and he certainly didn't want her to start making comments about Lucy. He hadn't seen Judy to talk to since before his date.

Judy looked at him quizzically. Was he being facetious? She

didn't think so. And she recalled her conversation with Lucy last night at the cinema where they had watched what turned out to be a tedious spy thing, totally incomprehensible. Judy had snorted.

'Barry?' she asked. 'Are we talking about the same Barry Swan we all know and love? He let you go home unmolested?' Lucy had been put out; she hoped it was because, old-fashioned as it might seem, he respected her. Judy made it sound as if the only reason he didn't try was because he didn't fancy her.

'He was quiet all the time really,' Lucy admitted. 'I think something at work had upset him.'

Well, Judy told herself, credit where it's due. The man's not a total pig. Maybe underneath that conceited, arrogant, overbearing exterior lurks a heart after all.

Now, as she agreed to go with him, she looked at him with kinder eyes. And then in the car he had to go and open his mouth.

'We all know about your feminist leanings, but don't let them affect you here, will you? There are women who aren't like you.'

Judy leant back in her seat and sighed. Typical. Give the man a chance and he has to go and blow it.

'My feminist leanings, as you put it, have never affected my work, nor will they. Naturally, the same can be said about you, your views don't affect your work. You don't have any. How can you when you think with what's in your trousers?'

She knew, she just knew she shouldn't have said it, but it was too late. He did it so often, set himself up as a sitting duck. She glanced sideways without moving her head. There was a bright pink spot of colour staining his cheekbone. Good, she thought, served him right.

'I could report you for insubordination.'

'Don't be so pompous. You could, but you won't. You'd be a laughing stock if you put that in a report.' That's what infuriated him most. She was usually right.

At that moment they drew up outside the Campbell's modest semi. The small front garden was neat and tidy, consisting only

105

of a paved path leading to the door and a square of grass. In silence they approached the front door. No lights showed although the dusk was turning to darkness.

Barry rang the bell. Almost immediately they heard a movement and Helen came to the door. Sergeant Swan introduced them. Helen's face blanched. She was right, something awful had happened to Alan. Her legs felt weak. She knew the form, there was always a female present when they brought news of death to another female.

'May we come in?' She nodded dumbly and led the way into the sitting-room. There, too, everything was neat and tidy. Magazines were in a rack, cushions were plumped up and the pot plants were healthy.

'Alan?' she stammered. 'Has anything . . .'

'Your husband's not here?'

'Not here? No, of course he's not.' She looked around wildly as if he might materialize.

It was Judy who first realized that not only was he not there, but he had not yet spoken to his wife.

'Sergeant Swan,' she said, 'I think we ought to wait . . .' but she did not know how to complete what she wanted to say. They had already caused Mrs Campbell more than enough anxiety. Barry saw how things were but realized they couldn't leave without some sort of explanation. Silently the three parties in the room appealed to each other for help.

'What's happened?' Helen said at last, her voice rising in panic.

'Mrs Campbell,' Judy said, 'your husband is quite safe. We thought, wrongly, I'm afraid, that he had spoken to you already. I'm sorry it had to come from us first. You see, Mrs Campbell, we're in possession of some pornographic videos in which you appear to have taken part.'

'Oh God.' Helen Campbell aged visibly and Judy could see what she would look like in ten years' time. 'I'd stopped, you know. It couldn't go on. I can't explain why I did it, but it's over. It's been over for several months. It took me ages to get the money they owed me. Alan knows.' The words were spoken with total finality. This was the reason he was avoiding her, why he couldn't even bear to speak to her on the telephone. She didn't blame him.

'I'm sorry to have to ask, Mrs Campbell,' Barry said, now the worst was over, 'but we have to know the names and addresses of everyone else involved.'

'Will I be charged?'

Barry shrugged. It was difficult to tell. A lot depended on what else they turned up. That was obviously not the only tape she made.

'I can't say for certain. Maybe not. Your co-operation . . .'

'Yes, I know all that, but I can't tell you, I swore I wouldn't.'

'You have no choice. If you're not prepared to speak to us here we'll have to ask you to come to the station, and that would make things a lot harder for your husband. There is also the possibility that child pornography may be coming from the same source.'

This had not crossed Helen's mind. 'No,' she said, 'George would never do that.'

'George who, Mrs Campbell?'

So she told them all she knew, describing how she had been approached by a girl she worked with and asked if she could do with some extra cash, and how she was put at ease with several large drinks. 'It was all done so professionally, nothing actually really happened, it was just made to look that way. The scenes were shot and reshot until it was all meaningless. I never even saw one finished.' Helen Campbell then named names and gave addresses but it was obvious she knew little of the operation except her own part in it.

Barry and Judy returned to the car, distressed by the incident. Mrs Campbell was well spoken, well dressed and loved her husband. She was extremely upset. They both knew from experience that appearances were often deceptive; some of the hardest, most mercenary vice girls lived in suburbia with husbands in business and children in private schools.

'It's a pity you didn't check with Alan first,' Judy commented, but without venom. She was equally guilty; she had not asked

107

Barry if he had done so. 'We'll have to tell him she knows that he knows.'

Barry nodded. They drove back to the station. Mrs Campbell had promised to come in and make a formal statement in the morning. If Barry or Judy were around they would try to make her visit as inconspicuous as possible.

They parked the car and walked up the two front steps. Barry headed straight for the vending machine and got two polystyrene containers of coffee, black, without sugar for Judy. She knew then that he did have feelings. By doing his duty he had probably put even more distance between a colleague and his wife. The whole business left a bad taste in their mouths.

Normally he would have expected Judy to run and fetch the drinks; this was his way of calling a truce. Each took a seat at a desk and manned a telephone. By early tomorrow morning everyone Helen Campbell named would have had their premises searched.

Neither felt like going home. Judy's flat was not a place in which she particularly liked living, but it was the best she could afford. Her father, whom she loved dearly, was always offering her her old bedroom back but she knew it would be a fatal move. Once back in his care, eating the good food he had learned to prepare when her mother died, she would lose the thin thread of independence which she clung on to and which he had taught her to value.

Barry's accommodation was far more luxurious. He owned a two-bedroomed service flat in one of the better parts of Rickenham. This was not due to his own efforts but to his paternal grandmother, a wealthy matriarch who, over the years, had fallen out with all of her children and bequeathed the flat to Barry in her will. All that was required of him was to decorate it in his own, more modern taste.

'I think I should go and see him,' Barry said when they'd finished making their calls. Judy knew who he meant. 'It's the least I can do.'

'Want me to come with you?'

He looked at her with surprise. She was being neither patronizing not contemptuous and for the first time since he met her he felt they were on the same side.

'Yes,' he said, 'yes, I'd like that very much.'

They left a note of their destination at the desk with Sergeant Whitelaw who was still on a run of night duty, and left. He glanced at the pair from under his heavy, sardonic brows but remined silent. Whatever he was thinking he kept to himself.

They drove across the town, Barry driving, and headed towards the run-down area near the station. Here buildings had been demolished to make way for new office blocks. The offices had not materialized. In their place were hoardings plastered with posters, many of them carrying the same advertisement for a band who had appeared at a venue in Ipswich on a date long past. Behind the hoardings were mounds of rotting mattresses amongst which the town drunks and down-and-outs slept. No effort had been made to move them off; they would only go to a site more obvious to local residents, who hated their presence but offered no assistance in housing them.

As they drove, a brilliant white light zigzagged across the sky, followed, seconds later, by a clap of thunder. Within minutes the temperature dropped several degrees and rain hit the windscreen in drops the size of hailstones. Barry flicked the wiper lever; dust and diesel grease and the remains of numerous insects smeared across the glass and momentarily obscured his vision. He pressed the washer button and speeded up the wipers.

'At last,' Judy said. 'I'd had enough of this bloody heat.' A siren sounded in the distance as if the rain itself was responsible for whatever personal drama was being enacted in another part of town.

They pulled up on the cobbled forecourt of the hotel, now shiny with water. The rain and the darkness went a long way to flatter its appearance, disguising the peeling paintwork and the threadbare curtains at the windows. Lights shone welcomingly through the open front door and the frosted glass of the saloon bar window. They went into the Station Arms and waited at the front desk.

On Sunday evening, fortified by several more gins, Tony Palmer got into his BMW and drove to Jacko's cottage. He was over the limit but he didn't care. How could such a system exist? One which was stupid enough to dictate how many drinks a person needed to make them incapable? He was used to the stuff, it took more than two to get him drunk. Besides, the police were too busy looking for a murderer to bother with him.

Jacko had returned from the hospital around lunchtime, bringing Janet with him. The boys were to stay with Dorothy Davies until evening. She said she would bring them back at bedtime. Janet was very pale but otherwise all right. The doctor had given her some tablets and told her to take it easy. He asked a lot of questions, not so much about her general health, but things like, was she under any strain. She had got off lightly with concussion, nothing that wouldn't right itself in a day or two. Once they were home Jacko insisted she went straight to bed. He took her up a cup of tea. She was still there when Tony Palmer arrived.

'Penhaligon? Are you there?'

Jacko didn't recognize the voice but he recognized the threatening tone. Slowly he went to the door. When things started to go wrong for him they usually continued to do so for quite some time. It didn't matter. All that mattered was that Janet and the boys were safe.

'Yes?'

'You horrible little bastard. Touching my kid. And now Sharon. I should've done this long ago.' The first punch glanced off the side of Jacko's head as he ducked away. The second made contact with his jaw. He fell to the ground, unaware that Janet, who heard Palmer shout, had come downstairs to investigate. She watched, horrified, as Tony Palmer kicked her husband in the ribs. In three strides she was by his side, hammering at his chest with her fists. Taken by surprise, he let her continue for some seconds before he grabbed her wrists. Unpleasant and bombastic as he was he would never hit a woman.

'Get out!' she screamed. 'Get out of my house and leave us alone.'

All the self-righteous bluster he felt in front of his own family drained away. What he saw now was an ill-looking woman trying to defend her husband. He wondered if Celeste would do the same.

Jacko groaned and rolled over and began to get to his feet. It would have been all right if he had stayed down, Palmer might even had apologized. But Jacko landed a resounding smack to the man's chin, and he wasn't having that. He retaliated with full force until Jacko was on the ground once more, blood oozing from his nose, one eye already beginning to close. Once he saw his opponent was helpless Palmer left, thinking how proud of him Celeste would be. 'Should have done it years ago,' he told himself again as he drove off.

Janet bathed Jacko's wounds, thinking what a fine pair they made. She didn't think he needed a doctor, and knew, in any case, he would refuse to see one.

'Enough is enough,' she said, drying her hands on a towel. 'I will not have my family persecuted. It's bad enough with the police without people like him.'

'Janet? Where're you going? You can't go out, you're not well, you know what the doctor said.'

'I won't be long. You sit there quiet. I'll get the boys on my way back.' Before he could protest further she had gone. He sat down to wait, in no fit state to do much else. Janet was a sensible woman; he trusted her to do the right thing.

When she returned and told him what she'd done, he began to doubt his opinion.

'I've been up to the hall to tell Mr Langdon you won't be in to work tomorrow, and I've also been to the police.'

'You've done what?' The boys, whom she had collected from Dorothy Davies at the same time, had never known their father to be in a fight and couldn't take their eyes off his injuries.

'And quite right too. Sergeant Davies'll be round to see you when he's had his supper. Don't matter what you've done or not done in the past – it's up to the law, not Tony Palmer, to sort it out.'

Jacko saw by the set of her shoulders that there was to be no argument. She began making their own supper, her injury forgotten, her anxiety overcome now she had something physical to deal with.

Sergeant Davies arrived just as they finished eating. He shook his head when he saw Jacko. 'It's one thing after another, isn't it? Janet told me all about it. Care to give me your version?' Bob Davies was beginning to think it would be easier to move in with the Penhaligons, he was seeing so much of them lately.

'Came to the door, he did, shouting his mouth off. Then he thumped me.'

'Tony Palmer?'

'Yes.' Janet answered for him. 'Jacko doesn't know him but I do because their youngest goes to school with Brian.'

'Palmer,' Bob said, his tone resigned. And he would bet he'd been drinking. Too late now, he'd been home some time, he'd simply say he'd had a few drinks when he got back. 'What did he say?'

'That he should have done it a long time ago. When, you know . . .' He didn't want to say it in front of his children. 'I know what he's thinking. He thinks I . . . Sharon, you know.'

'Maybe, but it still doesn't give him the right to do this to you. Have you seen a doctor?'

'No need,' Jacko grunted. He never went near them, it was bad enough fetching Janet from hospital with all those horrible smells and people in bed. It wasn't normal. Illness was something Jacko had managed to avoid and couldn't understand how people let it happen to them.

'Do you want to bring a charge?'

'No,' Jacko said, but Janet's 'Yes' was louder.

'This time we do. If Palmer gets away with it how long do you think it'll be before everyone else wants to do the same?'

'Jacko?'

'If the wife says so, I suppose I'll have to.'

112

Sergeant Davies took down the details, sighed wearily and went on his way.

Tony Palmer answered the door. The drink was wearing off and he no longer felt quite such a hero. Surprisingly he raised no objections to accompanying the police officers into Rickenham. Sergeant Davies was definitely off duty and insisted on having an hour or so he could call his own. Once at the station, Palmer was cautioned and charged. He informed the arresting officer he was only doing their jobs for them, then he was sent home to await the court case.

Meanwhile Jacko was discussing developments with his wife. 'I don't know what I've got us into this time,' he said, 'but as long as you're here I'll cope with it. I just hope they find Sharon's killer soon, then maybe they'll leave us in peace. I really thought you'd left me, you know.'

'I know, love. I expect they'll find him soon.'

Michael, whose presence they sometimes took for granted, was listening, without appearing to. His parents were the best in the world and he hated to see them unhappy. He knew what he must do.

It was still daylight and he was allowed outside until dusk during the holidays. Without saying a word he slipped out of the kitchen door and made his way to the mobile unit.

The two officers on duty there were not doing an awful lot. They had brewed some tea and were sipping this while they contemplated packing up for the night. They were surprised when Michael's head appeared round the door.

'I've come to tell you,' he said in his slow, careful manner, 'I killed Sharon.'

The two men looked at each other without saying a word. At last one of them said, 'All right, son, have a seat and tell us about it.'

Michael told them everything, from the time he went off to the woods up to the present moment. 'Thank you for telling us, Michael,' one of the men said. 'I think it might be a good idea if you came into Rickenham with us and you can tell the detectives there all about it. What do you say?' Michael agreed.

They knew the Chief wanted the boy questioned; his absence was explained by his mother's stay in hospital and his and Brian's sleeping over with Sergeant Davies. But why hadn't Davies questioned him whilst he had him in the house? Lack of communication was the cause. Bob Davies had assumed that whoever was questioning the children had seen Michael already and no one had told him otherwise. Bob might know everyone in the village but he was not telepathic.

'I'll have to let me mum know,' Michael said. 'I'm not allowed out on my own after dark.'

'We'll go up there first. In a police car. How'd you like that?'

Michael smiled. He'd like it very much.

They locked up the incident room, hopefully for the last time, and drove out to the Penhaligons' place.

When Jacko opened the door he could do no more than shake his head. He didn't think he could take any more.

'Mr Penhaligon, we're taking your son into Rickenham for a bit of a chat. He tells us he knows something about our investigations.'

'I'll go with him.'

'I think it might be better if you didn't, sir.'

'How will he get back?'

'Someone'll bring him if, well, unless . . . Don't worry, sir, we'll look after him.' He didn't have the heart to say he might not be coming back and Jacko was too stunned from the events of the day to protest. Janet had gone up to have a bath or she would have insisted she went with him.

'Michael hasn't done anything. That boy wouldn't hurt a fly.'

'Goodnight, sir. As I said, we'll take good care of him.'

Jacko laid a hand on his son's shoulder. 'Just tell the truth, boy. We'll see you later.'

'Look after mum, won't you.'

Jacko nodded. At that moment he felt he needed someone to look after him. He watched dumbly as Michael got into the back of the police car and was driven away.

114

7

The inquest was set for Tuesday morning. Everyone relevant knew where and when to turn up. Martyn Bright had planned to send a junior, guessing it would go according to the usual form, but when he heard that well-known phrase, 'someone was helping the police with their inquiries', he decided to go himself. Ian, too, hoped for the usual adjournment which would allow the body to be released for burial. Doc Harris had done a good job on the post-mortem; there were no unexplained injuries or toxins to warrant further examination.

It seemed ridiculous to the Chief that with all the facts to hand and all the computers at their disposal they had been unable to get anywhere. The cranks had all been ruled out. And then out of the blue, Michael Penhaligon had come forward and held his hand up. What he told them was not conclusive evidence, and his admission alone didn't count. Half a dozen other people all over the country had also admitted to the crime.

They kept Michael in the cells overnight. There was still plenty of time before they had to charge him, and with what the family had been through recently, it seemed kinder. Several people in Little Endesley had seen Michael being taken away. If he was returned again the same night it might mean more people knocking on their door demanding to know what was going on.

The whole business sickened the Chief. A death, and that of a child, was bad enough, but every stone they turned up revealed more dirt. Who was always on about a can of worms?

Swan, of coure, one of his expressions. Except that this time he was right. Sharon Vickers dead; the Penhaligons in never-ending trouble; pornography – and one of his own men's wives involved. Had it not been for the murder investigation, that mightn't have come to light. How many more worms would they uncover before the business was over? But not tonight, he told himself as he made his way across the car-park. No more tonight. A very quick pint then home to his wife and son.

As he unlocked the door of his Rover he saw a figure out of the corner of his eye. For a second he did not recognize WPC Livingstone; he had never seen her out of uniform. He was also not expecting to see her at that time as she came on duty in the morning. Now, with the make-up he had noticed earlier slightly smudged, her hair already beginning to show signs of grease and her very ordinary mufti clothing, he felt another pang of pity. She was the sort of woman no one looked at twice. Only her uniform gave her a sense of presence. She was undoubtedly intelligent and capable and would one day make one of the best policewomen, but she was not in the least attractive. She walked in his direction, smiling tentatively, and gave him a wave. He wondered where she lived and if there was someone waiting at home for her. Somehow he didn't think so. She was not another Judy Robbins after all. Judy could have had her choice of men but preferred being alone. She was a very self-possessed young lady, full of vitality. By comparison Pat Livingstone seemed half alive. Ian cursed himself for his pity when he heard himself ask if he could give her a lift somewhere.

'Thank you, I've love one. The top of the High Street? If you're going that way.' He was and she knew it. There was little she didn't know about Ian Roper. He stood for everything she admired in a man and he must like her, why else would he choose to sit next to her in the canteen and now to offer her a lift?

Ian intended having his pint in The Crown, the pub on the Green, just off the High Street. It seemed daft to drive past it, drop Pat and return. He invited her to join him. She accepted without hesitation. There was nothing underhand about such an invitation; officers of all ranks and both sexes drank together after work. They were colleagues sharing the same stress and often the same danger and needed such times to relive those moments. Brian Lord had once described it as spontaneous group psychotherapy, a way of getting it out of their systems before going home. Together they could talk for hours about 'the job' without inflicting it on their families. Now and again someone became too reliant on the drink, occasionally an affair developed, but these were the exceptions rather than the rule.

Ian pulled into a parking space at the side of the road, remembering not to be lazy and leave the car with two wheels on the actual Green. The residents were forever complaining. Their cottages were all under a preservation order as they, and the scrubby bit of grass they bordered, had formed the original Rickenham Green some two hundred years ago. In the middle of the grass was an oak tree surrounded by a wooden, slatted bench. This, and the trunk of the oak, were carved with numerous initials and hearts with arrows dissecting them. The verge of the Green was gradually being worn away and dusty soil spread inwards for a distance of about five feet.

Ian held open the door. Inside The Crown the air was oppressive. Cigarette smoke hung in a thin, blue canopy, unmoving, although all the windows were open. There was a peculiar stillness and the sky was tinged with yellow.

'What would you like?'

'Lager and lime, please. A pint.' Ian was not surprised at her request; he'd seen Judy knock pints back as if they didn't touch the sides.

He ordered the lager and his own beer. No matter how hot it was he would never, ever touch what he called 'foreign muck', sticking to Adnams, preferably not too chilled. Real ale was his thing, but Moira had trained him not to be quite so pedantic. There was a time when he refused to stay in a pub if the beer was under pressure. 'It's all right for you,' he'd told her, 'gin and tonic always tastes the same.'

117

'Cheers,' he said, handing Pat her drink. They found a free table as most of the customers had taken their drinks outside to get what little air they could.

'Do you think it's him, sir? Michael Penhaligon?'

'Everything seems to point to it,' he replied, falling into the trap of discussing work when all he wanted was to get away from it for a few hours. 'Don't you?'

She shrugged. 'I don't know. As you say, everything fits, but why didn't he come forward sooner? I know he's a bit simple – sorry, but you know what I mean, you can't be sure how his mind works – but I don't understand why he chose now.'

Ian forgave her her phraseology; it was so confusing now, not knowing what or what not to call anyone for fear of being labelled an 'ist' of some sort. Judy Robbins had quickly taught him the meaning of 'feminist' and 'sexist', and God help the future of procreation if every little girl grew up with her views.

'We'll have another go at him tomorrow. A night in the cells can do wonders. Nothing new in the village today?'

'No, all routine stuff, at least for me. The Penhaligons haven't had a good day. And I overheard two women talking about Harry Morgan. He's not been out of his house since yesterday, not even to take the dog out. I think I was supposed to overhear. They don't know about the videos but maybe they think he killed Sharon.'

'I suppose it could look like that to the local gossips. Bit of a smarmy character, lives alone with that poodle. Still, until we're one hundred per cent certain, everyone's a suspect – don't ever forget that, young lady. Everyone's suspect, everyone's lying.'

Pat had often heard the Chief's views repeated but it was the first time from the horse's mouth. She looked at him and smiled. The smile put him immediately on his guard; it contained everything she felt for him. Now he understood the make-up and the street clothes. It had happened once before, prior to his promotion. A witness to a burglary was forever at the station, bringing him new and useless information. He had had no intention of returning her obvious overtures and was annoyed that he had not been able to defuse the situation

118

sooner. He'd taken some stick over that episode from the lads; and he'd been so worried she might discover where he lived that he had told Moira.

'She's got the hots for you, that's all. I'm not the only mad one, after all.'

He was quite shocked at her bluntness and said he wouldn't have put it like that.

'Wouldn't you? What else would you call it? She hardly knows you so it can't be an appreciation of your brilliant mind or a shared love of real ale. She fancies you.' He never did find out if Moira was mocking him or, more basically, if she was jealous. He hoped it was the latter. He was not going to allow it to happen a second time, especially when it concerned someone with whom he had to work.

Ostentatiously he looked at his watch. 'If you want that lift we'll have to go now. My wife's expecting me.' Pat picked up her glass and drained it, unable to hide the disappointment in her eyes. No, Ian told himself sternly, you are not to feel sorry for her, it'll only lead to trouble.

He dropped her off at the top of the High Street, deliberately refraining from asking her where she lived, then drove on, across the roundabout, not feeling safe until he pulled up outside his own house.

Moira and Mark were playing Scrabble. Moira's mother had introduced them to the game and they were fast becoming addicted.

'No looking at my letters, now,' she said as she went to put the kettle on.

'We're nearly finished. Do you want a game, dad?'

He did not. He wanted to sit in his chair in the garden, which was now in shadow and might offer some coolness, or to sit in front of the television and watch some mindless rubbish which didn't cause him to think. He wanted to forget Sharon Vickers and the interlude with Pat Livingstone.

'Go on, then, I'll give it a try. I'm not very good at that sort of thing.'

'You do crosswords, don't you? Same sort of thing.'

119

Moira returned with three mugs of coffee.

'You two finish your game,' Ian said, 'while I have a quick look at the paper.'

'You haven't tried your shirts on yet. Why don't you do that first?' He had forgotten about his present. It would be ungracious not to do so.

'You look great,' Moira told him when he came downstairs to model the first one. 'It really suits you.' He felt pleased and quite youthful and wondered if they had been bought because Moira thought his style of dress a bit staid. Remembering the fifteen-year difference, he thought it might be time to get rid of the comfortable old jumpers he wore around the house and invest in something a bit smarter.

'Eight, and out,' Mark said gleefully. Moira shook her head. Her son had picked up the intricacies of the game far more quickly than she. He was able to fill in gaps with a couple of letters and make several words at once, scoring more than she could with a long word.

'Dad? Ready?'

'Yes, but not down there.' Unlike his wife and son, Ian was never comfortable sitting on the floor. They moved the game over to the dining-table and Ian realized what a long time it had been since they had shared any form of entertainment as a family. The concentration required to ensure he didn't finish in third place allowed him to forget the problems of the day, at least temporarily.

As they started playing the room darkened. Through the french windows black clouds were building in the sulphur-coloured sky. The curtains fluttered; lightning flashed, illuminating the garden; there was a clap of thunder then the rain started, beating down on the garden furniture like drum taps.

Sergeant Swan and WPC Robbins pushed the bell on the desk of the Station Arms. The lady who came in response to it told them Mr Campbell was in the bar. She followed them in there and took up her place behind it, her duties being twofold.

Alan did not seem surprised to see them. 'Want a drink?' he asked. 'Or are you still on duty?'

'No, we've knocked off. I'll have a lager. Judy?'

'Thanks – me too.'

Alan ordered and paid for the drinks.

'She knows,' Barry said after a long swallow of his drink. Judy nearly choked; he certainly wasn't messing around. 'We went to see Helen, about the videos. We needed names. She knows that you know.' He paused, not knowing how far he should interfere. 'She's very upset.'

'She's very upset, is she? Well, well, poor Helen. How does she think I feel?'

'You ought to go and see her.' It was Judy who made the suggestion. 'She told us she'd given it up some months ago.'

'And that makes it all right, I suppose.'

'She spent all the money on things for you.'

Alan refused to make eye contact with either of them, staring fixedly at his drink. 'How bloody kind of her.' The large whisky in his glass disappeared straight down his throat. Neither of them had heard him swear before, not even with a crowd of the lads, and it was something he thought should never be done in front of a woman.

'I'll drink to that,' he said, ordering another whisky. He raised his glass. 'To kind, caring, loving, Helen. And we all know what I mean by loving, don't we?' He sniggered and slid the glass over to be refilled.

Barry bought the round, watching Alan anxiously. He was drunk. Not one too many under the belt, not half cut, but very drunk, and he was a man not used to over-indulgence.

Before Judy and Barry finished the halves they'd ordered, Alan downed another whisky and, turning to say something to them, slithered off his bar stool.

'Young man,' the landlady admonished, 'it's time for bed, I think. I don't want any trouble. I don't want my regulars upset.'

Judy and Barry looked around. What regulars? There were only four other people in the barnlike place apart from them-

121

selves, and no wonder. All the other pubs in Rickenham at least looked in better nick than this one.

'We'll get him upstairs,' Barry offered. 'Sorry about this, he's got some family trouble. Which room is he in?'

'Number eight. First floor on the left. He's got his key in his pocket. He'll need to sleep that one off.'

They managed to get him up the stairs and took the key from the pocket of his jeans. The room was nothing special but after the condition of the bar, better than they expected, and it was clean. They undressed him and got him into bed leaving a toothglass of water on the bedside table and the waste-paper bin by the bed, hoping he would see it in time when the inevitable happened. As they closed the door he was already snoring.

'Just as well he didn't go to see her in that state. Anything could've happened,' Barry commented as they drove through the pouring rain back across town. 'Where shall I drop you?'

In the end he took her all the way home. She didn't ask him in and he didn't expect her to.

Monday morning was cooler and fresher. The rain still fell in sheets and the air smelled of wet tarmac. One or two country lanes were flooded and the council had put out warning signs. The ground was too hard for the water to seep away.

In Rickenham storm drains gurgled greedily and buses splashed pedestrians with murky water which ran along the gutters. The sky hung low and grey, the relentless heat of the past few weeks already forgotten.

The rain seemed to bring a kind of release. Mothers in Little Endesley slackened the reins on their children and allowed them out in twos and threes, as if murder was not an act that could be committed in a downpour. They still issued instructions: 'Only as far as the post office, mind,' or 'Ring me as soon as you get to John's house.' Only Ronnie Vickers refused to go anywhere. He wanted to stay with his parents, fearing that if he was out of their sight they would forget his existence. They remained huddled in the gloomy front room, biding their time until the inquest, hoping that tomorrow little Sharon's body would be returned to them and they could bury her. They were vaguely aware that all their friends were being interviewed, but what did it matter? It would not bring Sharon back. They could think of no reason why anyone could have decided to kill her.

'The reason isn't always logical,' Sergeant Davies explained when he called in to see how they were faring, 'not to the likes of us anyhow. But there always is one, a reason. We'll find him.'

Harry Morgan, pale and tired after two sleepless nights, returned to work. No one commented but they thought he looked as if his holiday hadn't done him much good. He did not think the police would turn up at his office, but he was wrong. He had only been there a few minutes when they arrived. They told him he would not be getting his videos back and they needed to know, must know, where he got them. He refused to say and was politely requested to come down to the station. He went to fetch his mac and umbrella. One of his partners cornered him in the cloakroom. 'If you talk, you're out,' he said. Only Morgan heard these words.

By the time he was seated in an interview room, a cup of tea going cold in front of him, four other men and three women were also being questioned. Using the list of names supplied by Helen Cámpbell, raids, organized by Barry and Judy the previous night, were carried out that morning, synchronized to the minute. The videos in which Helen took part were nothing to what else was discovered. Amongst many that were as harmless as those Morgan had in his possession, they found what they were looking for. Child pornography. And the equipment with which it was made. It was a good day's work but the men knew that, although a small vice ring had been broken, it was only a matter of time before another took its place. The euphoria of success was also overridden by the contents of the confiscated goods and the knowledge of what the children concerned had been through.

The Chief arrived to find a flurry of activity. There was more to come. A small working party was formed to deal with the children and their parents, some of whom would possibly know what had been going on. A child psychologist was brought in. Basically, however, the case was solved. The Chief left it in the hands of the working party and went to see Michael Penhaligon. Before he got there he received a message to say DC Campbell would not be coming into work. Barry had taken the call and naturally assumed it was because of the state he had been in the previous evening. He told him he would make it all right with the Chief.

'It's not that. Oh, God, what have I done? Helen's in hospital.'

For a split second Barry imagined Alan had woken up and gone to see his wife and, in his drunken state, knocked her around, and it would have been his and Judy's fault.

'I had to see her. I went first thing this morning. I knew, you see, I didn't want to lose her, whatever she'd done. If I hadn't gone . . .' He sounded close to tears.

'Take it easy, Alan, tell me what's happened.'

'Pills and booze. She'll be all right, though – fortunately there wasn't enough in the house to do the job properly.'

'Is there anything we can do?'

'No. Thanks, anyway. I'm at the hospital now. I'll try and get in later if I can. I've got to talk to her, get this thing sorted out. The job's nothing compared to her.'

Barry wished him luck and hung up. The Chief would insist he took some leave now, whether he wanted it or not. Better to be short-staffed than have somone making vital errors.

'What a mess,' the Chief said when he asked Barry to come to his office for a few minutes. 'Sharon gets killed and all these other lives are affected. Palmer was released on bail last night, by the way.'

'Yes, I know. At least we've cracked the porno case. At least those kids'll have a chance in life now.'

'Maybe. We've got the ringleaders, the ones producing and distributing the things, but I think there's still more out there. Too many people refusing to talk, and I want to know why. It can only be', the Chief continued, answering his own question, 'because they're protecting someone. Someone big, maybe, someone with clout. Even Morgan's saying nothing, and he's small fry.'

'It's a start though,' Barry said, trying to jolly the Chief out of his mood. He was not an easy man to work with when he got a bee in his bonnet. 'There are six children who won't ever have to go through that again. That's something, surely?'

'It might be too late for some of them. You know the routine. An institution, or foster parents, and ending up in prostitution. People really make me sick. Times like this make me want to give it all up and take a nice nine-to-five office job and let someone else deal with all the filth.' He meant it. He put his head in his hands and tried to imagine such things happening in his own family. He felt physically, as well as mentally, sick.

'Come on,' he said, 'let's go and have a word with Michael.'

On the stairs they bumped into Superintendent Ross. It was going to be one of those days.

'Ah, Roper, any headway?'

Ian gave him a brief run-down, adding, 'Though quite frankly, I don't think it's the Penhaligon lad. I can't say why.'

'One of your hunches?' Was Ian mistaken or was Ross smiling? The job really was getting to him. Ross never smiled. 'And the pornography?'

'Seven under arrest. Videos and equipment confiscated, but there's a few loose ends to tie up.'

'You've done a good job there. Broken the ring, by the sound of it.' If he was hearing praise from Ross, Ian thought he must be hallucinating.

'I'd like to get the lot. I don't want to think there's more of that stuff out on the streets. We've stopped this little operation, it's true, but where's the rest of the stuff?'

'Come now, Roper, don't let your imagination get the better of you. This is a local thing. You've already arrested seven people, it won't be anything bigger than that here in Ricken- ham. The case is closed. Wrap it up and get on with the Vickers murder.'

125

'Is that an order, sir?'

'Yes, Roper, it's over.'

Ross might think so; Ian did not. He decided to have another go at Morgan. For the time being he'd been allowed home. If his actions were queried he would say it was in connection with the murder.

Michael was brought up from the cells. He was terrified and burst into tears at the sight of the two detectives.

'There's nothing to be afraid of,' Ian told him gently. 'We just want to ask you a few more questions, to go over what you told us last night. Do you know what this is?' He indicated a recording machine on the desk.

Michael shook his head.

'When I switch it on it will record what we say. It makes it a bit easier for us to remember afterwards. Do you mind if I switch it on?'

Michael fidgeted then shook his head. He sat hunched over the table, an ungainly figure, his arms and legs clumsy. He hoped he would tell them the same things as he did before.

Ian switched on the machine, identified himself and those with him in the room and gave the date and time. Unknown to Michael, the police psychologist, Brian Lord, was seated behind a pane of two-way glass ready to make notes on his mannerisms and responses.

'Would you tell me your full name, please?'

Michael smiled. 'Michael Trelawney Penhaligon,' he said proudly, as he'd been taught.

The interview started. Michael repeated the story he told them the previous night. He was in the woods on Friday afternoon and he saw Sharon. He admitted his mother was not keen on him playing with her but he liked her. He also said his mum didn't like his dad talking to her, and he had heard her shouting at him about it. It was slow progress but eventually they arrived at the crucial time.

'Couldn't say exactly what time it was. I broke my watch, see, and I can't have another one until my birthday.'

'But it was afternoon?'

126

'Yes, after dinner.'

'Straight after dinner?'

'No, but before tea-time.'

'And what did you do, Michael?'

'I saw her.'

'Sharon?'

Michael nodded.

'You saw her. What did you do then?'

'I went over to her.'

'Did she say anything? Did you?'

'No, she didn't say nothing.'

'What did you do?'

'I put my hand over her face.'

'Show me how, Michael?'

Ian watched. From behind the glass Brian Lord leant forward in his chair.

Michael raised his right hand and held it, thumb uppermost, over his own nose and mouth. His large, calloused hand covered the lower part of his face. It would have been simple for him to smother Sharon.

'When you did this, what did Sharon do? Did she scream or struggle?'

'She didn't do anything. She just lay there.'

Everyone in the room stiffened. He had not said that last night. Just lay there? The Chief asked himself.

'You said she just lay there?' He had to be certain.

'Yeah.'

'Where?'

'On the ground. I thought she was mucking about.'

'And was she on the ground when you first saw her?'

'Yes, like I said, I thought it was a trick. She was funny, Sharon, she can trick me easy.'

'And you put your hand over her face. Why?'

Michael was confused, hadn't he told them already? 'It was a game. To frighten her, like what she does to me. You know, you put your hand over someone's eyes from behind. But she was facing up so I couldn't do that. I never meant her no harm.

127

Honest, she's my friend, I was only mucking about.' Michael's eyes filled up. It was difficult to know whether he fully understood the implications of the interview or if he was missing Sharon.

'Why didn't you tell us last night that she was already on the ground when you found her?'

'I thought I did?'

The Chief sighed. He believed him. 'OK. When she didn't respond, that is, when she didn't do or say anything, what did you do?'

'I went home. I thought she didn't want to talk to me. Sometimes she was like that.'

'And you didn't tell anyone you'd seen her?'

'No, mum might have told me off, and dad was out. Then I forgot. When dad was saying someone had killed her I knew it must've been me. I never meant to, though.'

'Do you know what death is, Michael?'

'Yes, you go to sleep and then you go to heaven.'

They couldn't charge him. The duty solicitor who witnessed the interview shook his head. A good defence lawyer would run rings around them. It was a no-win situation. His client said he killed the girl but no one believed he was guilty.

'We'll get someone to run you home, Michael.'

The tension in the room eased when the Chief spoke those words. The decision to release him had been his and his alone. No one else could be held responsible.

Back in his office, the Chief, with yet another cup of coffee in front of him, asked Sergeant Swan to nip down and see what was in the incident book for the previous night. He should have looked on his way in but he had had other things on his mind. 'And while you're about it – no, on second thoughts, don't.' He had been about to suggest they send some flowers to Helen Campbell but she was, at the very least, a witness in the pornography case, and possibly more.

Barry returned with the relevant information. Sunday night

was quieter than Saturday, but that was to be expected. A couple of breaking and enterings, one, in the Chief's opinion, totally justified, if such things could be. The householders had gone on holiday, not only forgetting to cancel their papers but also leaving the bathroom window open. Would people never learn? There was the usual list of petty crimes, which infuriated him. Perpetrated mostly by youths trying to gain a few quid without having to work for it, these crimes had a nasty habit of remaining unsolved. Such trivial thefts . . . What was wrong with civilization? No, he mustn't go off on that tangent.

The last entry Sergeant Whitelaw recorded before he went off duty was a little out of the ordinary and seemed senseless and malicious.

A hospital porter, rising at six a.m. to get ready for an early shift at Redlands Hospital, had prepared a bowl of tinned meat and crunchy biscuits for his German Shepherd and had then gone to fetch him in. The dog, whose uninspiring name was King, slept in the shed at the bottom of the garden. When his master was out he was kept on a long chain because he had a penchant for jumping over the fence and running off if left to his own devices. The shed was warm and dry and King had a blanket-lined basket. Jim Adamson saw no reason for keeping a dog in the house but he treated him well. He was fed regularly and given lots of exercise, but when Jim went to bed, King went out to the shed.

That morning there was no joyful response when he opened the door. King was lying in his own vomit, flecks of foam around his mouth. Jim saw at once he was dead but called the vet anyway. He would have given anything to have him alive again.

The vet told him he was of the opinion King had been poisoned and that he ought to call the police. He would take the dog away and do a post-mortem to confirm it and write a report. He had known Jim since the time King had had his first injections and his report would include the fact that he had been well cared for. He was aware of the long walks the two had enjoyed together, either before or after Jim's shifts. Perhaps

King had become noisy. Much as he loved animals himself, the vet knew what a nuisance a barking dog could be.

'Get someone to check it out, will you?' the Chief said to Barry. 'See if any of the neighbours have complained recently, anyone with kids the dog may have frightened, anyone who's complained about noise or fouling the footpath. Campbell can run it through his computer. Damn it, he's not here – well, whoever's free. And one more coffee, please.'

Barry went off to do his bidding, wishing the Chief would pull himself out of this mood. He didn't like being treated like a servant.

But the Chief was frustrated; nothing seemed to be going right. He should feel pleased with seven arrests in one day – it made the figures look good if nothing else – but he felt there was more to it. And Sharon. Three days into the case and nothing gained. Although he might have made a terrible mistake in letting Michael Penhaligon go, something told him he hadn't. There was nothing more he could do. Every spare man was employed in tracking down the killer. Every other force in the country also had the details. He would have this last cup of coffee and go and see Morgan. If he could satisfy himself that Ross was right he'd be able to concentrate better.

Sergeant Davies, who had eventually had a spare hour or two to spend with his wife on Sunday evening, had wasted it by talking about work. They agreed the Penhaligons were certainly going through a bad patch and that they never expected something so awful to happen in the village.

'I don't know love. I've racked my brains, but I can't think of anyone who'd harm the girl. There's one or two a bit on the bad-tempered side, and a few with strange ways about them, but to kill someone? Can't believe it's someone local.'

Sergeant Davies got on with his routine work on Monday morning. He did not know about the poisoned dog. Not then – not until much later, when it was all over. There was no reason at the time why he should have known; it was an isolated incident which had occurred in Rickenham Green. Had he known and told Dorothy in one of their confidential chats, it would have saved a lot of time.

Morgan, who had gone straight home after he was released on the Monday morning, sat with Suki on his knee. She was whining, unable to understand her confinement to the house. Morgan was scared and it showed. He sat in semi-darkness, the small windows not allowing much light in, the rain lashing against the leaded panes. There was a glass of whisky beside him. He sipped at it occasionally, letting it burn his throat, perversely enjoying the nausea as it hit his stomach. His rule, which had really been his wife's rule, was no alcohol before the evening. Then it might be a glass of sweet sherry for her, a large whisky or gin for Harry; that was quite sufficient before dinner. Afterwards Harry could have another if he wished, but Mrs Morgan drew the line at two. Excess of any description sickened her. In fact, looking back, he realized a lot of things sickened her. What would she think of him now? The owner of all those videos, and being questioned by the police? Drinking whisky in the middle of the day? 'How disgusting,' he could hear her say. In his mind he believed he had loved her. He must have, surely, to have looked after her all those years when she was ill? Coming home from work to cook her food and sit with her, and he'd kept his promise she wouldn't end her days in hospital. Was it really love or was it fear of change? There had been many times when he wished things hadn't disgusted her so much, wished he could make love to her with the light left on, wished they could have gone to one of his functions and let their hair down together without her screwing up her mouth in distaste if anyone became even slightly merry. And the television. How many years had he done without one because Enid Morgan thought it a vulgar thing? Morgan did not consider himself a vulgar man. He was well educated and enjoyed reading and good music but he could see no harm in watching the occasional bit of fun. He took another sip of his

131

drink. So early, and on an empty stomach it was quickly taking effect. He was a little confused, unsure whether the whisky was making him maudlin or whether it was enabling him to see things more clearly. He wondered if all those years of marriage were as good as Enid had led him to believe. He couldn't bear the thought that they might have been wasted.

None of it mattered now. He was still ten years away from retirement and about to lose his job. The senior partner would not want someone on the premises who was part of a criminal investigation and if he told the police what he ought to tell them, then Lloyd would ensure he got the sack – he was his immediate employer. There was no chance of another job at his age.

Harry Morgan decided to do nothing. He could not return to work in the state he was in; he might as well finish the bottle and write the day off. He was surprised to see it was already half empty.

When the door bell, another of Edith's whims, chimed its familiar notes, Morgan flinched. He hated it, the sickly notes of sentimental rubbish. He should have done something about it as soon as she died.

He staggered into the hall, for the first time aware of her influence everywhere. The flowered wallpaper, the little feminine touches. What had she turned him into that even after her death he left everything as she liked it?

Through the ridged glass panel in the door he recognized the tall figure of the Chief Inspector. There was a way out, a way of saving face so he wouldn't have to return to work where they might find out about the videos.

'Come in,' he said, hoisting Suki further up under his arm a little too roughly and causing her to yelp. 'Come in.'

He gestured towards the front door. Ian and Barry immediately assessed the situation. On a small table next to one of the armchairs was a half-empty bottle of Teacher's and a glass.

'We're sorry to trouble you again, Mr Morgan, but there are still – '

'It's no trouble,' Morgan interrupted, careful not to slur the 's'. What he'd thought of seemed a brilliant idea. If he admitted to the murder they'd lock him up, away from other people. He wouldn't have to worry about work or living or anything. Let the state take care of him. But who would look after Suki?

The Chief, when he heard what Morgan had to say, raised his eyes to the ceiling. Barry bit his lip. Another confession? What was going on in Little Endesley?

'All right, Mr Morgan. Give us the details, the how and the why.' The Chief noticed that Barry was half-heartedly taking notes. In all his days as a policeman he did not think he'd ever heard a less convincing confession. Nevertheless they listened to it. Because a thing did not sound convincing, did not mean it was not true.

'I can't stand children,' he said. 'They're dirty and untidy and Enid always . . .' He stopped, hiccuped and reached into his pocket for an immaculate white handkerchief. He'd just realized he was crying. 'I'm sorry, I don't know why I told you all that. I thought, you see, I thought . . .' and Harry Morgan told them what he had thought.

'Poor sod,' Barry commented as they drove away. 'His wife must've been a real harridan.'

Morgan, fired by the whisky, had poured out his heart to them. He spoke of all the years of living just the way his wife wanted, never doing any of the things that really interested him and then, after her death, almost like an act of rebellion, buying those videos and sitting in the bed where she died to watch them. He told them of his fear of losing his job, the position which brought him so much respect. Then he wondered how come, if he was so respected, he had no friends. By admitting to the murder he might at least gain some notice, even if it was notoriety. Pure fantasy, caused by the whisky.

'Yes, as you say, poor sod. Still he told us what we wanted to know. No wonder he was afraid to talk.'

Once more behind his desk the Chief looked at the list he'd made. On it were the names of the various staff at Bleasedale & Co., from the senior partner down to the lady who did the cleaning. Lloyd's name was third on the list.

'He's being questioned now, I take it?' Barry nodded. 'Quite an influential person in Rickenham. He's on the local council and sits on several boards. It'll be interesting to see what he has to say. If he's involved, you can bet there'll be a few more influential names.'

Lloyd was brought in but refused to talk until his solicitor was present. He tried to insist that a senior police officer interviewed him. He was full of self-importance and nobody's fool. They would have to tread very carefully with Lloyd.

'There's only one thing,' Barry said, wishing, too late, he'd bitten his tongue. 'What's the Super going to say about this?'

The Chief groaned. Officially the case was supposed to be closed. Still, he could hardly be reprimanded for adding to the arrests.

'I'll deal with Ross when the time comes. Now, maybe we can get on with things.'

Alan Campbell reported back on duty a few minutes after three o'clock. As soon as he heard Alan was on the premises, the Chief asked to see him.

'Don't be a bloody hero,' he told him. 'From what Sergeant Swan tells me, you've got more problems than you can cope with, coupled with the fact that you were on a bender last night. There's no way you're up to the job.'

'I'd rather be here, sir, if you don't mind. Now I know Helen's all right.'

Ian had to admit Campbell didn't look too bad – a little pale, but much more cheerful.

'You've spoken to your wife? About everything?' Tactful as he was, he did not want to give the everything a name.

'Yes. It's a thing of the past. And I've checked downstairs. The statements. That man George Bolton, who Helen thought was the boss, confirmed as much, he said she refused to go on with it. He was annoyed. He thought her being married to me was a sort of insurance, that I'd protect her, and consequently them, if things went wrong. I wouldn't have, sir, had I known.' Ian nodded. 'She's sick with worry about what's going to happen to her and how it'll affect my job.'

"Are you worried, Alan?'

'No, sir. I'll stand by her now whatever happens. The job takes second place.'

Ian wondered how he would have felt had the situation been reversed. The way he'd been feeling the last few days he believed he'd have said the same.

'I didn't know, you see. I didn't realize how she feels about herself. And I thought I was the one lacking confidence. She's so pretty, I never imagined anything could be wrong, you see.'

Ian did see; imagination was not one of Campbell's strong points. As to what would happen to Helen Campbell, it was not yet known. Her naïvity was unbelievable. She had seen no further than taking off her clothes and doing as she was directed, for which she was paid. What happened to the film afterwards was not something she had thought about, and it seemed likely she had not been aware of the full range of the operation. For the moment Campbell was his main concern. There was nothing for him to go home to, and the dreariness of the dark sky and sodden ground was not the sort of weather conducive to positive thinking.

'All right. You can put in a couple of hours, but I want you out of here by six at the latest. Is that understood?'

'Yes, sir. And thanks.' He might not be thanking him if his wife was charged.

Barry Swan reappeared, bearing two mugs of coffee. He had left the room when Campbell arrived. 'I don't know why we keep drinking this muck,' Ian observed as he sipped it. Barry tried to conceal a grin. The Chief, who drank more of it than anyone, complained the most. 'Highly amusing, Sergeant, but when there's no choice . . . For heaven's sake, Swan, not in here, my nerves can't stand it.'

Barry extinguished his cigarette, carefully knocking off the end so he could finish it later. Roll on the time when the Chief was back on the weed and they wouldn't all have to suffer. When Superintendent Ross first put them together as a team he was in the process of giving up and Barry thought they'd never make a go of it together. His new boss was short-tempered and

135

ratty. Barry naturally assumed this was his norm until Sergeant William Baker put him wise. 'Don't worry, son, it's always the same. The first three weeks are the worst. After that there's a stage when he nags everyone else to give up, then he becomes human. You just wait and see. Once he's convinced himself and everyone else he's kicked the habit, he'll start missing it and it won't be long before he's begging a fag off you.' Barry hoped he was right, it was making him edgy. Every time he reached into a pocket he was on the receiving end of a dirty look.

'Anything new?'

Barry shook his head. 'Not a thing. Sergeant Davies says everyone in Little Endesley and within a radius of several miles has been seen. No one knows a thing. It's beginning to look like an outsider.'

The Chief agreed. Media appeals to anyone who had been passing through had met with little response. It was not a tourist area and the industrial estates where salesmen might be calling were to the south-east of Rickenham. There was little reason for anyone who wasn't local to be in the village.

'But I can't see why. It's too . . . I don't know, too unlikely. Look at it this way. A stranger, for whatever purpose, happens to be in the village. He, or she, stops their car and takes a walk in the woods. If they parked some way off and walked, from whichever direction, someone would have noticed them. OK, they might have fancied a stroll after a long, hot drive, but they wouldn't know who else would be in the woods – and why should they suddenly decide to kill an unknown child? I could understand it if there'd been a sexual motive, but there wasn't. It doesn't seem logical, does it?' The Chief's questions were rhetorical but he wished someone could provide the answers.

Knowing that the men under him were quietly and efficiently following up the minutest pieces of information as they came to hand, the Chief turned his attention to his in-tray. A big case was underway but this did not prevent smaller crimes being committed. They, too, required investigation. He glanced at a couple of files and put them aside for later; a third should not be on his desk at all. He was irritated, it was perfectly plain it was intended for the boys on Drugs. There was so much delineation now, but if they wanted it that way, someone should be responsible for keeping it that way. He rang downstairs and gave the filing clerk an ear-blasting.

Amongst the papers were notes on Jim Adamson's case, or, more accurately, King's case. No one in the vicinity of Deben Road, which was Adamson's address, was recorded as having registered a complaint. That, in itself, didn't mean much. Someone could have been bending Adamson's ear for months without calling in the police. He slung that, too, to one side. He'd get a beat bobby to make a few inquiries. It was bound to be a neighbour.

'Oh, sod it. All right then, Barry,' Ian said, sighing in exasperation. 'Give us one of your fags.'

Barry Swan offered him the packet. He didn't say a word, but inside he was singing hallelujahs.

8

Moira took a plate of multi-coloured salad from the fridge, unpeeled the plastic film which covered it and placed it in front of her husband. She said she was surprised to see him home so early but was glad, because she and Mark were just about to eat.

'Is it over?' she asked, when she'd reminded him not to leave his car keys on the dresser but to put them on the hall table or he'd spend an hour looking for them.

'No, not by a long way. We don't seem to be getting anywhere. Where is Mark anyway?'

'Watching television. Mark!' she called. 'It's ready.'

'I just want to watch the end of this,' he shouted back.

Moira decided not to insist, salad would keep. Ian picked up his knife and fork and began to eat, for once making no comment about rabbit food, and helped himself to dressing. Moira, passing behind his chair to get a jar of pickles, knew immediately why her lack of culinary effort had received no criticism. She smelled the smoke on his clothes and in his hair, but she could not smell beer on his breath so it hadn't seeped into his clothes in the pub. She did not object to his smoking, although the house was fresher when he stopped – it was what they had to go through each time he gave up. Now was not the time to mention it. If it was enough to start him smoking again, the case must be getting to him.

'I've just about had it,' he told her through a mouthful of grated carrot. 'The whole thing's beginning to get me down. It never ceases to amaze me what people'll do for money, and there's Ross breathing down my neck every five minutes. Sorry, didn't mean to go on about it. I needed to get away for an hour or so, I'll probably go back in later.'

'Ross? What's up with him now?' Moira had met him once at a police ball. She had disliked him on sight, finding him supercilious and patronizing. When she heard that his wife had left him she merely commented with a sniff, 'I'm not in the least surprised.'

'A pornography case. He told us to wrap it up before we were half finished. That man doesn't live in the same world as us mortals. He can't get it into his head that Rickenham Green is no longer the quaint little market town it was when he first came here. It's like everywhere else, the more people, the higher the crime rate and the worse the crimes.'

Moira said nothing, letting him get it out of his system. She might get indigestion but at least he wouldn't keep her awake talking about it.

The Chief was more bothered than he was letting on. Ross had telephoned late in the afternoon demanding to know why his orders had not been followed. 'I told you this morning, Roper,' he said, 'the case is closed. I don't imagine you'd like to find yourself on a disciplinary charge?'

'No, sir, but you have to admit there's more to it than we first suspected. Lloyd, for example – he was selling in bulk in London and Ipswich, and you know the sort of stuff it is. What he was selling locally was a drop in the ocean. We could hardly let it rest there, sir.' Ian put his case as tactfully as he was able.

'Chief Inspector, if I say the case is closed, then it is. Leave it to the city boys to clear up.' And with that Ross had hung up.

He had a point. The producers and distributors were on their patch but they were under arrest. The other forces involved had been supplied with all the details; it was technically up to them to do the necessary. Ian did not like the thought that, few though they might be, there were hard-core videos circulating locally. Why should a handful of people get off free just because they were a handful?

Lloyd was being held in the cells and Ian had a good idea bail would be refused. He wanted to see him personally, not because he distrusted the men who had interviewed him, but because he had a hunch. This was not a foolproof method of detection by any means, but hunches had come off before. Now, after an hour or so with his family and with a meal inside him, he would have a psychological advantage over Lloyd who had never been arrested before and would not be seeing his family for a long time.

'Lovely,' Ian said as he mopped up the garlic-flavoured dressing with a slice of bread.

Moira looked at him. He wasn't being sarcastic. You couldn't win them all, but if his smoking meant he was prepared to eat healthier food, that was something.

She picked up the plates. 'Mark! If you don't come now you won't get anything.' With Ian home early she could get all the dishes out of the way in one go. Mark came into the kitchen and with an exaggerated sigh sat down to his meal.

'Evening, sir,' the desk sergeant said, automatically pushing the incident book across the desk as the Chief walked towards him. 'Looks like it's clearing up a bit out there. Might be nice tomorrow.'

'Mm. It's stopped raining.' Ian glanced down the page. Nothing much. It was too early for real trouble. Another fire. He could never understand why so many buildings managed to burst into flames during wet weather. A student nurse had reported a prowler, or what she suspected to be a prowler, outside the nurses' home. Ian knew how often Peeping Toms were found in hospital grounds and the nuisance they caused to the nurses. The National Health Service curtains, often shrunk by numerous washings, rarely met completely across their windows. A voyeur, if he waited long enough, could hardly fail to get a glimpse of flesh. The girls themselves didn't help. They often had their lights on long before it was necessary because they were not paying the bill.

'Who's patrolling the Weirside area this evening?'

'Stone and Jackson, sir,' the duty officer replied after checking a list.

'Get them to keep an eye out around the Rickenham General area, will you?'

'Already done it, sir, as soon as the call came in.'

'Good man. Thanks.' It might be a trivial thing but occasionally voyeurs were not content with just looking. Over the years more than one nurse had been killed when they came off a late shift or were returning to the nurses' home after a night out. There was no harm in checking.

That same evening, as the Casualty sister, Margaret Price, came off duty, she saw a man lurking in the trees which lined the short drive to the main hospital entrance. It was not quite dark but the low clouds made vision through the trees almost impossible. She hesitated, decided not to go and ask him what he was doing, and walked briskly out on to the pavement. Probably the man was waiting for someone in Casualty and had come out for a quiet smoke, or he might be someone's husband, come to meet his wife from work.

Margaret Price was not a nervous individual, more than one doctor could attest to that, but she was sensible enough not to risk walking home alone in the dark. Her quickest route lay through narrow lanes and the tail end of an industrial estate. This was fine in the summer but now she realized it would only be a matter of days before she would have to start using the car.

Her colleagues found it strange that she chose to walk over a mile each way when she was on her feet all day. That was tiring, but it was a different sort of movement from striding along at a good pace filling her lungs with what passed for fresh air. The walk gave her a chance to forget the odours of incontinence and vomit and death. She was an observant woman, as she was trained to be, and wondered why no one else noticed that many nurses were overweight. She knew her theory was correct; stepping from one patient's cubicle to another sapped one's energy but did not provide proper exercise, and after such a day, many nurses headed straight for the canteen and consumed greasy food.

It was dark by the time she reached home. Tomorrow, then, it was back to the car. She had her latchkey in her hand as she approached her front door, another of her sensible precautions, and took a quick look over her shoulder to see that no one was near. She went inside and turned on the lights.

As she made her supper she briefly remembered the man in the trees but forgot him again as she tossed a few salad vegetables to go with her pasta. She settled down to watch a film she'd pre-recorded over the weekend, unaware that the man's presence had already been reported to the police.

PCs Stone and Jackson, a team of long standing, patrolled their area conscientiously. Several times they made a detour past the grounds of the hospital and stopped to take a look around. They saw no one who was not walking purposefully up or down the drive, but the man had seen them. He knew they were getting nearer, might even realize his intentions. He had not waited all this time to be picked up for loitering, to have people think he was some pervert hoping for a glimpse of a nurse as she undressed. His intentions were quite different. He was satisfied, he need not come back again, he knew the pattern now.

He walked back to where he had left his car, feeling uncomfortable in the damp, evening air. It wouldn't be long now.

The Chief, finding a detective who seemed to have nothing better to do than sit on the edge of his desk and exude charm into the ear of what was obviously a female at the other end of the telephone, asked him if he could leave his courting until later and accompany him down to the cells. DC Emmanuel, very black and very handsome, said, 'Sure, sir,' and hung up, amused at the Chief's old-fashioned vocabulary. Courting was hardly the word he'd use to describe what went on between himself and Amarilla, who was all woman.

The Chief wanted to speak to Neil Lloyd. Superintendent Ross could hardly object to that – he had already been arrested.

Lloyd was not forthcoming. He repeated what was already on record. He sold the goods, using business trips as an excuse for his journeys. At first Ian listened patiently, then he and DC Emmanuel used the hard-man, soft-man aproach, a routine most detectives pick up quickly, like two well-rehearsed actors.

Of Harry Morgan, Lloyd only said contemptuously, 'That little creep. Sits at home on his own watching the stuff. I don't look at it myself, I just flog it to those who do.' Did that make it better or worse, the Chief wondered.

They tried the 'It'll be better for you if you talk' line, with no promises of a reduced sentence, but Lloyd could read that into it if he was stupid enough. He wasn't. They might be experts at interrogation, they might know all the angles, but Lloyd was equally up to it. He was playing games with them.

'I know the extent of my crime,' he admitted quite candidly. 'I knew the chances of getting caught when I started. Unfortunately, my dears, I have a very demanding wife, a lady who appreciates the good things in life. Even with my position in the firm I couldn't keep up with it. I do not offer this as an excuse for my behaviour, merely as the reason for it. The lady in question is not only demanding, she is, although it isn't any of your business, unfaithful. Again unfortunately, I happen to adore her. In return for what I provide she is prepared to stay with me and put up with my clumsy advances. C'est la vie. However, as you've both tried so very hard to extract information from me which I'm not willing to give, and have shown remarkable patience without causing me to "fall over" in my cell, I will, by way of compensation, give you one name.'

The Chief mentally bit his tongue. Was there a veiled threat in Lloyd's words? Was he the sort to inflict an injury on himself and then say he'd been brutalized? Emmanuel said nothing either. He simply pursed his sensual lips and narrowed his

143

eyes. They were being made fools of, admittedly by a man of equal intelligence, but it was not a feeling they much cared for. But a name. One could make all the difference. It might be that Lloyd would demand to see his solicitor or someone senior to Ian in the morning and say he'd been harassed, but they needed that name. It did not help to know that this was the type of criminal who appealed to Ross. Someone who was articulate and well educated, one who was not physically involved but made the money. Ross was a snob where his criminals were concerned.

'The name, Mr Lloyd?'

'Ah, yes, the name.' He paused dramatically. 'James Quentin Ross. Perhaps you've heard of him?'

Ross! The name resounded like a death knell in the Chief's head.

DC Emmanuel, whose pen was poised to write it down, froze.

'And what can you tell us about James Ross?' the Chief asked, trying to sound unconcerned.

Lloyd held up a neatly manicured hand. 'I said a name. You, after all, are the detectives. Now, if you'll excuse me, gentlemen, I think I've had enough for one day.' It was as if the man was in his own home and was politely letting guests who were overstaying their welcome know that it was time to go. The Chief and DC Emmanuel did so.

'Boy!' Emmanuel said when the door clanged shut behind them, a more appropriate phrase not springing to mind. 'What are you going to do, sir?'

'I'm not entirely sure. I think, certainly for this evening, we'd best keep this to ourselves.'

Winston Emmanuel was disappointed. What a story to tell the lads, and he'd been there to hear the words spoken! He knew the Chief's reputation. He was a man who expected confidences to be kept and discipline maintained. In return he treated his men fairly and generously. Winston would not let him down.

Ian sat at his desk watching the scum form on the tea he had carried back with him from the machine. His mind was on the dilemma of how to tackle the problem. James Quentin Ross was none other than the Superintendent's brother. He was also a well-known, successful barrister. These facts were relevant to the way he played it, but not so relevant as Ross's insistence that the case be dropped. There were two possibilities. Either Ross believed what he said about it being sewn up as far as their division was concerned and that Ipswich and the Met should tidy up the pieces, or he had known about the whole thing all along and was protecting his brother. And that meant criminal charges and an end to his career. Ian did not want to be the one to bring the man down.

He sipped the tea and almost spat it out, forgetting how long it had been sitting on his desk. 'Coffee,' he told himself. 'Another cup of the filthy stuff and then I'll think this thing through.'

He got the coffee but thinking became no easier. He had to inform Ross of the information Lloyd had given them, or someone had to. If he tackled him himself and Ross was innocent, it would save red faces all around. Ross could then go to the Chief Constable and explain the situation. If he was guilty it would give him a way out, the chance to resign before he was kicked out. On the other hand, shouldn't a matter of such gravity be dealt with by someone superior to himself? And oughtn't he to report it immediately? The coffee, too, went cold before the Chief came to a decision.

For the third night in a row Lynn Morris lay in bed unable to sleep, but by now Rob was aware of it.

'What's the matter, love? I thought we'd sorted everything out, that it was all all right between us now? You're lying there stiff as a board.'

'Nothing's the matter. Really. I'm just a bit tense.'

Rob got out of bed, the sick feeling he'd had over the past year returning. 'I'm going to get a drink. Want anything?'

'Tea, if you're making it.'

At the door he stopped, dreading to ask the question which was on his mind. 'Are you missing him? Is that what's wrong?'

'Oh, no, Rob. It's not that. I hardly ever think of him.' It was true, she didn't, not half as much as she'd thought she would. If only Rob would believe her.

'I don't understand, then. You tell me it's over yet you're worse than before. I can't get near you. Is it me? Is it something I've done?'

She shook her head. She wanted to tell him, to confess to the last meeting with John so that everything was above board, but if she did so now it would make everything else seem like a lie. This could not go on. She felt more guilt about not going to the police to tell them about the man she had seen than she had over the affair. She would call in at the police station tomorow. Once it was off her mind she could give Rob her full attention and things would get back to normal. She managed a weak smile. 'No, it's nothing you've done. Hurry up and come back to bed.'

Sharon Vickers' inquest followed the usual form, as expected. The Coroner made the hearing as brief as possible, pointing out that Mr and Mrs Vickers had suffered enough through constant exposure to the press and having to read about their daughter daily.

Doc Harris gave his evidence concisely and couldn't wait to get outside for a cigarette. A verdict of murder by person or persons unknown was given and Julie Vickers, once she heard that Sharon's body was being released for burial, broke down. Her own body heaved with great, shuddering sobs. 'At last,' Tom Vickers said, 'at last.' They could start the long, slow recovery now.

The Chief did not attend the inquest and sent Sergeant Swan along as his representative. Had they had any concrete evidence to produce he would have been there himself.

At eleven thirty, the second cigarette of the day in his hand, the Chief answered a call from reception which told him there was a young woman downstairs wanting to see whoever was in charge of the Vickers case. Lynn Morris was shown up to his office immediately.

'I don't know how to put this,' she began hesitantly. 'I mean, it's probably nothing, I just thought . . .'

'Please, have a seat, Mrs Morris. Now take your time, there's nothing to get nervous about. Anything you know, or think you know, no matter how silly it seems, could be important.'

She told him she had been in the woods on Friday afternoon and her reasons for being there. She had seen a man, not that that was unusual, but he seemed to be in a hurry.

'Was he running?'

'No, not exactly running, but walking very quickly. And he was carrying something. I couldn't see what it was but I got the impression it was heavy. I think that's why he couldn't go any faster.'

'How big was it? Whatever he was carrying?'

'About so big, I think.' Lynn held her hands about two feet apart. 'I'm only guessing, but whoever he was looked as if he didn't want anyone to see him, or perhaps what he was carrying – it was hidden by his jacket.' Now that she had started talking about it, she was surprised how vivid the memory was in her mind, considering the occasion for her own presence there.

Could the man have been carrying the child's dead body? Maybe Mrs Morris had her own problems too much on her mind to be accurate about the size. And she was very nervous. It showed in the way she sat on the edge of her chair, her knees pressed tightly together, and in the way she picked at her nails.

'What made you decide to come to us now, instead of sooner?'

'It was keeping me awake at night. Things were getting better between Rob and me and he didn't know about that last meeting. I thought it would all come out and he'd never believe a word I said again.' The Chief noticed those nails were badly bitten.

'Your domestic problems are your own affair, Mrs Morris, but we'll have to speak to John Williams. If you saw something, he might have too.'

She looked like a startled deer as she said, 'Oh, please, no. He couldn't have seen anything, he went the other way.'

'He might not have gone immediately back to his car. In fact, after hearing what you had to say he may well have walked for a bit. His address, please, Mrs Morris.'

She had no option but to give it to him but prayed he would not use this as an excuse to contact her again.

'Now, can you give me a description of the man you saw? Any particular details which stuck in your mind?'

'He wasn't young. I don't know how I know that, but I'm sure he wasn't. Maybe it was the way he held himself, or walked, or something. I know he was carrying whatever it was, but he just seemed like an older man. He was a long way off, I didn't see his face or the colour of his hair but it wasn't blond, I'm certain of that. It was a bit gloomy in the woods after the sunlight, my eyes hadn't quite adjusted.'

'Did you notice what he was wearing?'

'Ordinary things. Darkish slacks and a jacket.'

'Slacks? Not jeans?'

'No, they definitely weren't jeans.'

'And a jacket? Wasn't it very hot on Friday?'

'Yes.' She thought for a second or two. 'That's what made me think he wasn't young. Lots of older people wear jackets all the year round, don't they?'

The Chief nodded. 'If you could spare a little more time, Mrs Morris, I'd like you to look at some photographs to see if you can identify him.'

She assented, although neither believed it would do much good. Lynn had only seen him briefly, and then not his face. The Chief had already come to the conclusion that whoever did it had no previous record.

As Lynn Morris went through the albums of pictures, the Chief wondered if she was genuinely too upset to have taken notice of the man or whether it was John Williams, her lover,

148

they were after. If she knew he'd done it she might be trying to confuse them with a different description. She had had four days in which to warn him of what she intended doing, time enough for him to fix himself an alibi. No, it didn't add up. She claimed she and Williams had parted when she saw the man. If that was not true it meant she was a witness to the murder and, although she was anxious about her own position with her husband, she was far too composed to be hiding such knowledge. And why would he want to kill Sharon? Passion, maybe? Perhaps Mrs Morris had not gone to end the affair and the child had found them in a compromising position. For her sake, to prevent discovery, he killed her. Far-fetched? Yes, but he'd come across more fantastic motives than that in the past. He left her to continue looking at the photographs and went off to arrange for someone to go straight round to see John Williams.

Lynn went home with an easier mind. She had done the right thing and hoped she had been useful in some way. There was no reason for the police to ask Rob any questions. She kept her fingers crossed that that was the end of the matter.

And so, Ian summed up later that day, we have an unaccounted-for man hurrying through the woods carrying something fairly heavy. Could be someone quite innocent. Detective Chief Inspector Roper did not think so.

John Williams, they knew by then, was not the murderer. He and Mrs Morris had met early in the afternoon. At the earliest time possible for Sharon's death Williams was already back at work. Ian was wrong about his taking a walk. He returned immediately to his car and headed back to Rickenham. Mrs Morris had been walking for about fifteen or twenty minutes when she saw the man, her car being parked some way away, and he was in a hurry. God, he must have only just done it. A minute or two earlier and she might have prevented it. But she had not seen the child, alive or dead.

The wheels of routine continued to turn. Tuesday evening came round, the rain clouds having disappeared and given way to a pale blue sky in which cotton-wool clouds chased one another. As the shadows lengthened, the clouds, stationary now as if preparing to settle down for the night, were tinged with pink round the edges. It would be hot again tomorrow.

Ian wanted to go home; he was disillusioned and defeated. And there was that other thing hanging over him like a cloud far bigger than any up there in the darkening sky. It must be seen to at once – he'd already left it twenty-four hours. He had tried, he must give himself that. A junior officer was one thing – it was bad, but now and again they did get a rotten apple. For someone in Ross's position it was unthinkable. It would make headline news and all the efforts made at improving the relationship between the police and the public would be wasted.

If only he could walk out, go home to his wife's cooking and let her soothe his fevered brow. He was about to call Ross again when his internal telephone rang.

'Thought you'd want to know, sir,' the disembodied voice told him, 'PCs Stone and Jackson have been called to the home of a nurse from Rickenham General.'

It meant nothing to the Chief, who had far bigger things on his mind. 'So?' he inquired impatiently.

'Last night, sir, there was a prowler at the hospital? Stone and Jackson went to have a look?'

He remembered now.

'Well, someone's been and put a petrol bomb through her door.'

'Whose door?'

'A Casualty sister. Miss Margaret Price. One of her neighbours called the fire brigade then us, then the hospital to let her know. When Miss Price got home she also remembered seeing someone hanging around.'

'Anyone hurt?' This was indeed serious, could even be attempted murder.

'No, she lives alone and, as I said, she was on duty at the time.'

'I'd better come down. Give me a minute or two.'

The Chief dialled Ross's home number again. He had not

returned any of his calls and was nowhere to be found. There was no answer, nor from his car phone or his pager.

Ian took the stairs two at a time and almost collided with Sergeant Baker, who was clutching a bundle of files to take to the storage room. 'I might need you, Baker. Dump that lot and come back here.'

'Yes, sir.' William Baker was used to the abrupt manner of his boss when something important was up.

There wasn't much more to discover than what he already knew from the telephone conversation. Margaret Price was with neighbours when she was interviewed. She was told the fire appliances arrived so promptly that most of her possessions had been saved and damage kept to a minimum. If her neighbour had not spotted smoke so quickly it might have been a different matter. She was heart-broken. All her working life she'd saved and eventually put together enough for the deposit on her stone, terraced house. Even now she had to be careful with money, the mortgage repayments taking a good proportion of her monthly salary. Over the several years she had lived there she had managed to buy one thing at a time to make it home. There were also her mementoes from grateful patients or their relatives. Now half of it was ruined, blackened by smoke. At least the insurance would cover the cost of redecoration. But it was her home, the only real one she'd ever known, and it would never feel the same again.

The Chief Fire Officer said there was no doubt it was a deliberate act of arson. The Chief decided to leave it to the men already on the scene; he didn't need Sergeant Baker after all. The immediate neighbours had seen no one suspicious, but they might learn more when everyone in the street had been questioned. Margaret could come up with no ideas and thought the idea of an ex-patient, or a relative with a grudge, a ridiculous idea. Naturally there were people who died in Casualty and there were occasions when people made a fuss, claiming others had been seen ahead of them. Usually they were satisfied when she explained that the more serious cases were seen first. The

151

occasional late-night drunk might get a bit obstreperous, but would have forgotten about it anyway in the morning. She could not think of anyone who would wish to harm her.

Only then did she remember about the man in the trees.

'Do you think he had something to do with it?' she was asked.

'I shouldn't think so. I didn't really see him, but he didn't look familiar. More than likely he was waiting for someone, or hoping to get a look at one of the more nubile nurses.' She indicated her own body as if no one in their right mind would be interested in it. The interviewing officer thought there was nothing wrong with Sister Price, although she was a bit too old for him. She'd kept herself trim and tidy and wasn't at all bad-looking.

She tried to describe the man. He was their only lead. 'Not very tall, a bit hunched up, but that could have been because of the weather, not because he didn't want to be seen. Not young. Nothing outlandish about the way he was dressed.'

'You saw what he was wearing?'

'No, not really, it's just that if he was a punk or hippy or whatever, I'd've noticed. Just ordinary trousers and a jacket. You keep on about him – do you think he's responsible for doing this to me?'

'It's a possibility. How are you fixed for sleeping arrangements? Is there a relative or someone we can contact for you?' The house would not be habitable for several days. The kindly neighbour said not to bother, she would put Maggie up for as long as was needed, and Margaret preferred to be near to organize the workmen.

The Chief learned all this when Stone and Jackson arrived back at the station. He decided to sit it out until he could get hold of Ross.

'Seems like another dead end, sir,' PC Jackson said. 'We saw everyone in River Street. Usual story, no one saw a thing.'

River Street was quite a busy thoroughfare; it was used as a short-cut to the dual carriageway, and residents complained about the traffic. The houses were all terraced, with no front gardens, consequently most people drew their curtains as soon as electric light was needed to prevent passers-by from peering into their windows. Many had been in their kitchens having their evening meal or engrossed in the television. There was a pub on the corner and an Asian grocery shop opposite, which meant pedestrians were up and down the street all the time. Someone must have seen something. Another public appeal would have to be put out. Whoever did it must have been cool. And why then? If they wished to harm the owner, surely it would have been better to wait until she was in bed asleep. Or was it a message of some sort? If it was, no one was able to interpret it.

Ian eventually gave up. Ross was deliberately avoiding him. He had given him enough chances; he would have to go higher, but it was too late tonight. He would see to it first thing in the morning or his own position would be at risk.

'What a goddam awful week,' Ian said as Moira placed his meal in front of him. 'One thing after another.'

She sat and sipped a glass of wine as she watched him eat. His appetite did not seem to diminish no matter how trying work was. To try to lighten the mood, she told him how Mark had been out sketching most of the day and had produced a superb water-colour of the bridge and the river. 'Even the dog roses are exactly the right shade. I don't know where he gets his talent from, do you?'

Ian did not reply. She knew his mind was still elsewhere. She didn't mind; she knew it took a good half-hour before he was approachable. He pushed his plate away and wiped his mouth with a napkin before patting his shirt pocket. The comforting bulge was there. Moira, out of a habit she thought she'd forgotten, reached behind her for the ashtray and passed it to him.

'Thanks,' Ian said.

Moira smiled. Yesterday, she guessed, he'd bummed one or two cigarettes from a colleague, today he'd gone out and bought his own. There was one thing for which she was thankful: he had not returned to his pipe. It was not so much the implement itself she objected to, it was the stuff he used to burn in it.

'What we have,' Ian told her, apropos of nothing, as he leant back in his chair and exhaled a lungful of smoke, 'is the murder of a child, a senior police officer possibly on the make, numerous unsolved minor crimes, and some not so minor, and now an arsonist. Not the usual empty building, insurance claim syndrome, but the private house of a Casualty sister at Rickenham General.'

'I forgot to ask you, what happened about Ross?' The mention of a senior police officer had reminded Moira. 'Did he come down on you like a ton of bricks? I never could stand the man.' This was an exaggeration – the only time she had met him was at the police ball but her dislike increased every time she heard his name.

'Ah, well, no.' He had not told her of his suspicions. He was loyal enough not to discuss such a confidential matter even with Moira, whom he trusted more than anyone. 'I think he's avoiding me.'

He refused to say any more and she didn't press him. Astutely, she realized the senior officer Ian was referring to was Ross. She cleared away his plate, leaving it to soak in the sink, and poured them both another glass of wine.

There was a tremendous din coming from upstairs. It was not something they suddenly became aware of. Mark had been gradually turning up the volume of his cassette player, hoping his parents wouldn't notice if he introduced them to it slowly. He failed in his efforts. Moira took one look at her husband's face.

'It's all right. I'll see to it.' She went upstairs and hammered on his door.

'Turn that row down, will you? Your father's had a hard day and it's not doing me much good either.'

From inside came a few muffled bumps then the volume was reduced minimally.

'Come on, Mark, be sensible. More than that.' He did as he

154

was asked but did not bother to come to the door. Moira was annoyed. Over the past two years the boy had moaned continually about the way his father treated him. It was fair to say Ian had not realized his son was growing up, but a relationship worked both ways. Ian was doing his bit – it was time Mark made an effort, not just when he wanted attention.

She knocked on the door again. 'Let me in. I want to tell you something.'

She waited while he came to the door. She did not know what he got up to in there for hours on end, and, quite honestly, preferred not to. He was fifteen, almost a man, and, apart from one shoplifting episode, had managed to keep out of trouble. One or two of his acquaintances had not been so fortunate. He didn't smoke, although she knew he'd tried it, and she kept a vigilant eye out for any signs of drugs. She let him know she and Ian loved him and, without putting him in the charge of a bodyguard, felt she was doing the best she could to ensure he remained healthy and happy and kept out of trouble.

Mark showed great artistic promise and hoped to become an artist one day. That was fine by her. If he had talent and was able to use it in a career he enjoyed, no one could ask for more. She just wished the next year or so would pass quickly. Adolescence was a pain to go through, but it was equally hard for the people who had to live with it. She couldn't wait for the time when her son reverted to the smiling, even-tempered person he once was. How Deirdre, her friend, put up with it was beyond her. She had four teenage boys.

'Look, you know dad's home,' she said. Mark was already taller than her and would probably be as tall as his father, but it was her looks he had inherited, the blond hair and fair complexion which nonetheless tanned well, and the natural slimness. Of course, he had not yet filled out, he might end up constantly battling against extra weight, but she didn't think so. His neck was slender, not quite so bull-like as Ian's.

'Does he want me for something?'

'No, Mark, he doesn't *want* you for anything, but it would be nice if you at least came down and said hello.'

155

She saw his expression change. 'I'm listening to this.'

'Well, you can come back and listen to it in a minute. Come on, be fair, he's tried hard with you lately.'

Mark made a face, but with a hint of the old grin around his mouth and eyes. 'All right. I'll come and see how the old codger's doing.'

Moira playfully clipped him around the ear, not enough to hurt, but enough to disturb his carefully arranged hair.

'Mother, you know I hate that.'

She laughed, amazed anew at the vanity of modern youth with their hair gel and facial scrubs. They went downstairs and Moira was pleased at the effort her two men made with each other.

Barry Swan was out when the Chief decided to go home. He returned to the station with the intention of catching up on the Vickers case. He envied Ian; there was nothing he would have liked more than to go home. He also took a look to see what else was news.

Something caught his eye. A phrase he had heard before. It was a tenuous link but he had to check it. 'Ordinary trousers and a jacket,' Margaret Price had said. So had someone else. Who? It was twenty minutes before he found what he was looking for.

Lynn Morris. No wonder it hadn't come easily to mind. He had not been present when she came in and he'd only skimmed through the notes on her interview.

'Ordinary things. Darkish slacks and a jacket,' Lynn Morris had said. It was ridiculous, Barry told himself; hundreds and thousands of people wore slacks or trousers and a jacket. He did himself. But there seemed something relevant there. He made a note to speak to the Chief about it in the morning and left it on his desk to remind himself. What else could he do? He could hardly send men out to interview every man not dressed in jeans or a kilt.

He felt tired, not so much physically, but in the way Ian did,

156

with the fatigue of dealing with a case which was going nowhere. He wanted some company but could not decide which of the many females listed in his diary would best suit his mood. He found himself dialling Lucy Phillips's number, surprised to find he didn't need to look it up. He was equally surprised when she told him she was having a night in and was going to do her nails and finish a book she was reading. She did not say she had other plans or wanted an early night because of having to be up early. That hurt. He found it difficult to believe any girl would prefer those occupations to spending time with him.

'Please yourself,' he thought after he hung up. 'There's plenty more women out there.' What really annoyed him was that he had meant to ring her sooner, to aplogize for the lack of time on Friday night and to ask her out again. It was now Tuesday; from her point of view it couldn't have been very flattering. He sat for a moment or two taking stock. Was it anger he felt, or disappointment? He went to the door to make sure no one was lurking in the corridor to overhear his conversation, then he rang her again.

'Sorry to disturb you again.' He was nervous, not a feeling he was used to when it came to dealing with women, but he didn't think he could stand a second rebuff. 'I should've asked just now. If you're busy tonight, how about tomorrow, or the day after?'

'Well, just a minute.' Lucy was not playing hard to get, that was not her style. She was just wondering whether it was wise to get involved with someone whose reputation with women was as bad as Barry's. On the other hand, she had enjoyed the couple of hours they spent together.

'All right then. What time and where?'

For the first time in his life Barry experienced what he'd only heard other people talking about, the feeling of intense pleasure and relief in knowing the girl you were asking out wanted to go. Usually he took his enjoyment as and when he could find it, with little thought for the emotions of the person involved. He was good-looking, reasonably well off and had his own place. He never had any trouble pulling, as he called it. His aura of total confidence also helped.

'Eight,' he said. 'I'll pick you up.'

'No, I'd rather meet you somewhere.'

'The thing is, we're still on a murder inquiry. I don't intend to be late, but I don't want you to have to hang around somewhere if I should be delayed.'

Lucy hesitated. Perhaps she should change her mind. It was bad enough waiting for and being let down by Judy, who was her best friend – could she put up with it from a man? At least she knew what she was letting herself in for. Letting herself in for? What was she thinking about? She was only going on a date! She gave him her address and said goodbye.

Barry went out to his car and started the engine. He wanted to find the nearest motorway and drive up it at a hundred miles an hour. Instead, he curbed his excitement and, keeping within the speed limit, took himself home.

While he was waiting for the microwave to do its worst with a frozen dinner another thought struck him. There were two coincidences. Apart from the description of a man's clothes, the ordinary jacket and trousers, there were also two incidents, on two consecutive nights, involving hospital staff. One at Redlands and one at Rickenham General. Were they connected, or was the man seen hanging around nothing to do with either?

The microwave pinged and Barry placed his meal on a tray, along with a bottle of HP sauce and a can of lager, and took it through to his small lounge. He placed the tray on the coffee table.

He was sure there was a connection, only he couldn't see it. He went through it again. A man, fitting the same description, seen in two different places. Three different crimes, each concerning people who seemed to be Joe Average citizens who knew of no enemies or anyone who wished to harm them. And yet . . . Something in their past maybe, a vendetta?

Leaving his meal to congeal he rang the Chief at home.

'I think you may have something,' Ian said, not minding that his evening had been disturbed. Any idea, any lead was better

158

than the present situation. 'But what's the common denominator? We'd better start with the hospitals. Get your jacket on, son. I'll meet you at Rickenham General in, what, twenty minutes?'

In the car-park they exchanged a few words. There were two hospitals involved, but many of the Rickenham General staff had been transferred from Redlands when the new hospital opened in June. However, they met a blank wall. It took some time to rouse someone from Administration but it only took a few minutes to ascertain that Sharon Vickers had never been a patient there, neither had her parents, not even out-patients.

'She'll probably have notes at Redlands, the child. It's more than likely she was born there, especially if, as you say, they lived in Rickenham at the time. We only get Redlands records when patients are transferred to us, or if they come here to Casualty.' There was no longer an Accident and Emergency Department at Redlands. Eventually it would house geriatric patients and an X-ray and physiotherapy Out-patients clinic. 'Meanwhile,' the administrator continued, 'as and when people become ill they're admitted here and their records follow them. It was the easiest way of making the changes.'

'Thank you for your time,' the Chief said. 'You've been very helpful.' This was not strictly true but the man had been dragged away from whatever he was doing at home and it always paid to keep in with such people who could, when it suited them, be obstructive.

Barry and Ian returned to the car-park. 'Nothing much gained from that little visit. At least we know Margaret Price did work at Redlands – the connection, if there is one, has to be there.'

'Now, sir?'

Ian looked at his watch. 'No, it can wait until morning. It was hard enough finding someone here and as they're both part of the same health authority, it's an even money bet they have the same administrator. Fancy a drink?'

Barry thought of his chicken dinner. It had looked soggy enough when it was hot and steaming. He knew he wouldn't eat it now. A couple of pints with the Chief, then he would get himself a meat Madras, a nan and some onion bhajis. His mouth watered at the idea.

'The Crown or The Feathers?' Ian asked.

'The Feathers,' Barry said. He preferred their lager.

9

By Wednesday Jacko's injuries were on the mend. Gerald had insisted he take a few days off, refusing to let him stay when he turned up on the Tuesday. Jacko, unused to being idle, set off on Wednesday morning grimly determined not to be turned away again. He gained some satisfaction from the knowledge that Tony Palmer had been charged. For once the law was on his side.

Margaret Price, on that Wednesday, did the opposite. At very short notice she took several of her leave days to supervise the cleaning up and renovation of her home. She knew how lucky she was; had she been asleep she would have stood no chance – the banisters were already beginning to catch when the fire appliances arrived. In all her seventeen years as a Casualty sister she could not recall an incident when anyone had seriously threatened her, no occasion when anyone had had reason to bear her a grudge. Once, quite a few years ago, a man had quietly said that they would all pay, but she had forgotten this. She watched, as men arrived with ladders and paint, and decided to put it down to the work of idiotic youths. There were enough of them in Rickenham nowadays.

The Chief and Sergeant Swan arrived at Redlands Hospital just after nine o'clock, by which time the clerical staff were present. Their offices were still in a state of upheaval. Boxes of files were being sorted out ready for despatch to Rickenham General. The last thing they needed was interference from the police.

They waited patiently until Sharon Vickers' file was begrudgingly placed before them, listening to the buck passing as to whose responsibility it was to find it. She was indeed born at Redlands, eight years ago. It was an uncomplicated birth, both mother and child being strong and healthy. She was admitted for a tonsillectomy two years ago. It was all very straightforward and she was allowed home after a couple of days.

'Mrs Bryant?'

Mrs Bryant gave the Chief a withering look through her bifocals. 'We are extremely busy, as you can see. What is it you want now?'

'I apologize for taking up your valuable time. All the changes must make life difficult for you, but we are investigating the murder of a little girl.' The Chief was the epitome of charm and tact. He had dealt with officious, self-important women like her before. Mrs Bryant softened fractionally. 'But can you tell me, would Sharon Vickers' Out-patients notes be included in this file?' He was humouring her, pretending ignorance against her expertise in the filing system of the hospital. What he really wanted to say was, 'If you're so bloody busy, woman, why didn't you bring me both files at the same time?' He knew Redlands' idiosyncratic system. Other hospitals had patients' details in one place, and nowadays duplicated on computer – not so here. Separate records were kept for the two departments. And the Chief knew she must have had an Out-patients appointment with ENT before they whipped her tonsils out.

'No. Do you wish to see the file?'

'If it's not too much trouble.' The smile belied the intended sarcasm of the words.

'It was a good idea, Barry,' the Chief said as they made their way back to the station, 'but there's nothing there to connect Sharon to the other cases.'

Sharon was not one of those accident-prone children. She had never attended Casualty where she or her parents might have come into contact with Sister Price, and at the time of her operation Jim Adamson had been on leave. There was still the

162

point that both Price and Adamson had been at Redlands together for over ten years and had both been on the receiving end of personal attacks.

Back in the office the Chief tried every conceivable place to try to locate Ross. He knew then he had given him enough chances. He rang the Chief Constable's office.

He was thinking about the consequences of his action when a call was put through to him from a Mrs Barbara Jones, a neighbour of Jim Adamson's.

'I didn't know, you see,' she told the Chief. 'Not until this morning when I bumped into Mr Adamson. I was away until last night, down to my sister's in Aldeburgh.'

'Mrs Jones, let's start at the beginning, shall we? First, your address.'

She told him and took a deep breath. The Chief broke in before she could launch into her story. 'You live two doors away, is that correct?'

'Yes. And I saw him, the man what poisoned poor old Jim's dog.'

The Chief took a deep breath himself. If she was able to give a good description they might be getting somewhere.

'Now, take your time, tell me only what you can remember exactly.'

'I was putting out the rubbish on Sunday night ready for the bin men in the morning. It's always a bit of a rush Mondays, getting Bill sorted out for work, and I was going to my sister's for two nights, so I wanted everything good and ready, and – '

'Thank you, Mrs Jones. What exactly did you see?'

'Him. The man. To save Bill the job, I wheeled the bin down the garden and put it outside the back gate. We have to do that now, not like the old days. I don't know what we pay poll tax for – still, they're doing away with it, aren't they, and a good job too if you ask – '

'That's when you saw the man?'

'Yes. I'm sorry, my Bill always says my tongue runs away with me. He didn't come as far as my gate, so he must have stopped either next door or at Jim's, but I didn't hear anything, so it must have been Jim's. He'd've been in bed by then, he was on early shift.'

'What time was this?'

'About eleven thirty.'

'Did you get a good look at him?'

'Not really, he was turning away. But he wasn't all that tall, a bit shorter than my Bill – I'd say about five foot nine. I couldn't see his face clearly, it was dark apart from lights from people's windows, see, but he wasn't no youngster. He was wearing a jacket and dark-coloured trousers, and he walked with a bit of a stoop.' Mrs Jones waited in vain for praise for her powers of observation.

'Anything else you can remember?' It was a description of sorts, very vague, but it did match. 'Would you recognize him if you saw him again, Mrs Jones?'

'Oh, I don't know about that. I could try though. Did you want me to come down and look at some mug shots?'

Despite her choice of words, he was not in a mood to find them amusing. He didn't think it would do much good, but arranged a time for her to come to the station. There was always the slimmest chance it was someone on the books.

They now had three sightings of what might or might not be the same man. It was not so much the clothes, it was also the way he was described as being old, or at least not young. He made a few notes but was interrupted again by the internal telephone. Sergeant Baker informed him that Margaret Price and Jim Adamson only knew each other through work but had not met since her transfer. When she was at Redlands she called him Jim; he called her Sister. They did not mix socially at all and even in the canteen never sat together. The usual unwritten laws of hierarchy were obeyed there, as in any institution. Sisters sat with other sisters and staff nurses, students sat in chattering groups, and domestic staff and porters shared tables.

'Thanks, Sarge. Let me know if anything else turns up.'

'Yes, sir. Oh, and DC Campbell's put in a request for leave. Knowing how things work around here, it probably won't get

to your desk until tomorrow. Thought I'd let you know.'
William Baker was never the last to hear what was going on in
the station. He was liked and trusted and often confided in,
partly because he was a genuinely good-hearted man but also
because there was a touch of old-maidishness about him. He
thrived on gossip and scandal but never passed it on. It was
enough to know first, to be able to say later, 'Fancy, I thought
everyone knew that.' Alan Campbell's problems were common
knowledge, but Sergeant Baker was the first to hear his wife
had been transferred to the psychiatric unit for observation
because Alan himself told him. Sergeant Baker also distrusted
secretaries, not that he had one himself, of course, but they
were civilians, they didn't always realize how important small
things could be. At least the Chief had been warned he'd be a
man short.

Alan wanted to be at home when his wife was released from
hospital on Sunday. But Sunday was still four days away. The
Chief hoped by then the case would be solved.

'How's it going?' Dorothy Davies asked her husband when he
popped home for something to eat at lunchtime on Wednesday.

'It's not.' Bob Davies sat at the kitchen table and scratched his
grizzled head. He picked up a doorstep sandwich and bit into
it. Beside his plate was a pint mug of strong tea.

'Everyone's still talking about it. It's causing a lot of suspicion
– people around here can be quite vicious.'

Dorothy joined him at the table, bearing a plate with a daintier
sandwich and a cup of tea.

'I saw Mrs Black again today. She still looks awful, said she
feels worse now than when it happened.'

'Delayed shock,' Bob informed her through a mouthful of
corned beef and onion sandwich.

'Still, like she was saying at the bingo on Sunday, at least we
know Old Man Blake does eat properly. It's just more gossip,
that's what it is. He just gets all his tinned stuff delivered from
the post office so's he doesn't have to carry it. It's only because

165

he won't mix that one or two are saying he killed little Sharon. He's on a pension like lots of people, it's cheaper to get everything else in Rickenham, like his meat. We saw him in the butcher's.'

'Saw him?'

'George Blake. In the butcher's. Bob Davies, don't you ever listen to a word I say?'

He did, but at times there were so many of them it was hard to keep track. 'Sorry, love, I was preoccupied. I know the lads at Rickenham think I'm just an old has-been but this time I've got what they call a hunch. Nothing I can pin down, I can't see the who or the why, but I'm convinced someone from the village killed Sharon.'

Dorothy was so surprised she stopped chewing. She had never heard him use the word hunch before. Bob always said he believed criminals were caught by logical thought, by putting two and two together and making sure it came to four, and by using technology. Whatever next?

She removed their plates, brushed the crumbs from her husband's uniform and decided, now that the sun was shining again, to tidy up the already neat garden. She took great pride in it, saying that gardens reflected the personalities of the people who lived there. It did not compare with Mr Morgan's for colour – Dorothy preferred a real country garden look and grew old-fashioned stocks and delphiniums and Canterbury bells even though the police house was a modern, red-brick affair which looked out of place amongst the local stone cottages.

'See you later,' Bob said, kissing her cheek. 'I don't know what time. I think I'll make a few inquiries of my own. I'm going to pay a visit to young Darren Hargreaves.'

Sergeant Davies did not bother to take the car. The Hargreaves lived only a few minutes' walk away. Overhead the sky was the same unbroken blue as it had been a few days ago and there was a sleepy afternoon stillness, a heavy somnolence in the air only felt on hot days in August. He was sweating by the time he reached their front door. He knocked hard. If they'd seen him, which no doubt they had, they would pretend to be out. It was a ritual they went through every time he called. He could wait, he knew the form. He also knew every town and village had them, a Hargreaves family. They were the first people you looked to whenever a petty crime was committed. Breaking and entering, stolen cars, missing charity boxes, these were their speciality. But this lot weren't very bright; they usually left enough evidence around to make witnesses superfluous.

The house was not nearly large enough to accommodate the family, but usually one or other was in prison so they coped. And they'd turned down the chance of a larger one in Rickenham. At the moment Jack Hargreaves, the senior member of the family, was away looking for work, or so his wife was putting it around the village. Rumour had it he'd taken all he could stand and run off with a barmaid from Frampton. He'd done similar things before but always returned when he ran out of money or the girl got tired of him, whichever occurred first. His wife was a scraggy little thing, with thin mousy hair clinging miserably to her head. She seemed unable to speak in a normal tone of voice and was either bemoaning her fate in a high-pitched whine or screaming shrilly at whichever members of the family were at home at that time. There were five offspring, ranging in age from nineteen to six. The two oldest boys had been in trouble times too numerous to list. The third child was a sixteen-year-old girl, already pregnant and refusing to name the father. Bob's guess was that she didn't know who it was. The fourth, another boy, was considered odd by his siblings because he was doing fairly well at school and hoped to get a good job. The baby, six-year-old Samantha, was spoiled rotten by the lot of them.

It was Darren he wanted a word with now. The break-in at a nearby farm had his hallmark written all over it. He banged the door harder and shouted through the letter-box, 'Come on, open up. Don't you get tired of this game?'

167

He knew they were at home. A radio had been blaring when he walked up the short path, picking his way around a rusty tricycle and several unhealthy-looking bags of rubbish.

Lilian Hargreaves opened the door, wiping her hands on a filthy apron.

'Well, what do you want this time?'

'Is Darren in?'

'No.' She started to close the door but was not quick enough. Bob Davies had placed his foot in the door as soon as she opened it.

'Look, Lilian, I know we have to go through this charade every time, but I've still got a job to do. Go on, get Darren down.'

Lilian Hargreaves sniffed her disapproval, wiped her hands again and screamed up the stairs, 'Darren, get down 'ere. The police wants you. And don't pretend you're not there, I've already said you are.'

Darren appeared at the top of the stairs and stomped sulkily down.

'Yeah?' he said as he inspected a tattoo on his forearm. 'What now?'

'Just a few questions, Darren. Here? Or shall we go inside?'

Darren jerked his head towards the front room. Sergeant Davies, on entering it, wondered if it was a wise decision. The room was in its usual disarray, papers spilling over from every chair, dirty cups scattered around, their saucers doubling as ashtrays. The television was on, although the sound was down. He switched it off without asking permission.

'OK, son, Deacon's Farm. Last night. Care to tell me about it?'

'Don't know what you're talking about.' It was like a play, Bob thought, the same lines repeated time and time again.

'Pantry window broken, things knocked over on shelves and, guess what, a dirty great footprint on the windowsill.' He looked pointedly down at Darren's boots. There had been enough mud around after the rain to get a good print. 'Nothing taken, so the sentence'll be light. How about it?'

'Wasn't me.'

'I suppose you cut your hand shaving.' Bob had not failed to notice the sticking plaster across his knuckles.

'Very funny. I was here all night. Ask me mum.'

And a fat lot of good that would do. Lilian Hargreaves would swear blind to anything her sons told her to.

'I'm fed up with this,' Darren whined. 'Every time something happens it's always me, isn't it?'

'Yes. Usually. Or your brother.'

'You leave him out of it, he wasn't with – '

'I think we'd better start again, hadn't we?'

'God Almighty, your lot were only round here on Saturday. Can't you leave us alone for a moment?'

'Saturday was a different matter, a bit more serious than this. We saw everyone in the village, not just you. And don't forget, little Sharon wasn't much older than your Samantha.'

Darren blanched. The thought of anything happening to his sister was unbearable.

'Yeah. All right. I was fed up, like. The old man's buggered off again and we've got nothing coming in except what we get from the Social. I didn't get anything, though.'

'It's still breaking and entering. You'd better come along and make a statement. Come on, son, don't look like that, you should be used to it by now.'

'Can't we do it here?'

'Nope. You know we can't. Needs two of us. We'll go over to the mobile unit, someone there'll oblige.'

Lilian Hargeaves slammed the door after them, muttering something about pigs under her breath.

'Why does it always have to be me?' Darren asked as they strolled along. 'Why not pick on someone else, like that funny old bugger who's always skulking round the woods? And Samantha's school that time.'

'Which funny old bugger are you referring to?'

'I dunno. Lives round here somewhere. And he was up there on Friday when that kid was killed.'

Darren could have bitten off his tongue. Sergeant Davies

stiffened. Friday. The Hargreaves family had sworn they were all at home watching the racing on television on Friday afternoon. Not that anyone took what they said seriously.

They had reached the unit. 'Someone got a minute to take a statement? Young man here's held up his hand to the break-in at Deacon's Farm. First, though, perhaps he'd like to tell you about Friday afternoon. Go ahead, Darren.'

WPC Livingstone and her companion looked at Darren with interest. The lad had a shifty appearance and wasn't any too clean, but was he a murderer? You never could tell. Pat Livingstone prayed he was, that she could be the one to give Ian Roper the news.

'Why did you lie about Friday?' Sergeant Davies asked once the formalities were over.

'I dunno. I didn't know what was going on at the time and Benny wasn't around, I thought he might've been up to something.' Benny was the next boy down. What Darren was saying was probably true, the whole family protected one another.

'So neither of you was at home?'

'Don't know if he was but I wasn't.'

'What were you doing in the woods?' Darren Hargreaves was not the sort to take a walk for no reason. His head was bent but they could see by the red tips of his ears he was blushing. 'Come on, better to get it out in the open.'

'I was following her. Emma.'

'Emma Foster? I see.' Bob was aware of the relationship between Emma and Davey Harrison, but he was not aware that Darren fancied his chances in that direction.

'Don't know what she sees in him, stupid git, she'd do far better with me. I could show her a thing or two.' That, Bob Davies thought, was a matter of opinion, and the sort of things Darren was likely to show her were not everybody's cup of tea.

'Do you normally go round spying on her?'

'It's not spying. I just wanted to see what they got up to.'

'You could be in serious trouble, son. You've already lied to us once. Now tell us everything you saw and did on Friday afternoon.'

Darren had been buying cigarettes when he saw Emma and Davey and on the spur of the moment decided to follow them. He was jealous and he hoped to catch them at it and embarrass them, show Davey Harrison up. But he couldn't do it. He followed them as far as the top of the woods and realized what a fool he might look. It was on the way back that he saw the man.

'I don't know him, mind, not his name or anything. But I've seen him up there before so he must live around here.'

The man's description was what sealed it. He had known all along it was someone local. There were one or two others who also fitted that description, but Sergeant Davies felt certain he knew who it was. Darren was sent on his way, his lesser crime, for the moment, forgotten.

Detective Chief Inspector Roper received a call from the Chief Constable's office in response to the one he had made earlier. His presence was requested at a meeting the following day. His heart sank. If he'd dropped Ross in it without justification he was in all sorts of bother, but deep down he knew it was the right action to take. What he needed now was a breakthrough in the case – that should help soften whatever was coming his way.

He summoned Barry Swan to his office. They would go through it one more time.

'I'm certain you're right. It is a vendetta of some kind. These people are being punished. God, how stupid we've been. We've been asking why Sharon Vickers should be a victim. It's not Sharon, it never was. It has to be her parents. Price and Adamson have had the things they treasured the most destroyed – surely that's what happened to Mr and Mrs Vickers? Come on, let's go.'

They jumped into Ian's car and he let the Rover have its

171

head. 'There might be more people involved. We've got to find out.'

'Come in,' Julie Vickers said, her eyes puffy and red from crying. Ronnie sat in front of the flickering television screen, seeing nothing.

'Is your husband here?'

'Tom's upstairs, sleeping.'

'Would you wake him, please?'

'Must I? The doctor gave him some sleeping pills. I don't think he's closed his eyes since Thursday night.'

'Please, Mrs Vickers, it's very important.'

Julie did as she was bid. She returned with Tom, who looked dreadful.

'Sorry to wake you, sir, but we're looking at this from a different angle and we need to ask you a few more questions.'

Tom nodded wearily. 'I don't mind, if it helps catch the bastard who did that to my Sharon.'

'We feel there might be a connection between Sharon's death and two other cases we're investigating, but so far the only common denominator we have is Redlands Hospital. We know Sharon was born there and that she had her tonsils out, but is there anything else which connects you to the hospital? Anything at all?'

Tom shook his head, lack of sleep and the pills making it hard for him to concentrate.

'None of us have ever really been ill,' Julie volunteered. 'I went there for ante-natal care, and Sharon you know about – '

'No!' Tom Vickers shouted. 'No, it can't be.'

The Chief closed his eyes. This was it. He knew it. Whatever Tom Vickers was about to say he was going to lead them straight to the killer.

'Tell us, Mr Vickers, and we'll decide whether it can be or not.'

'It was before we got married, back in 1982. I lived in Rickenham then. It was a summer evening, just like the night Sharon died.' He was speaking faster, wanting to get to the end, knowing, as the Chief did, he could lead them to the murderer. 'A child, yes, an eight-year-old child, ran out in front

172

of my car. I didn't see her – I wasn't speeding, but I didn't see her. I didn't stand a chance of missing her.' Tom Vickers wiped his eyes on the back of his sleeve. 'She ran straight into the road. A cat. She was chasing a cat. I braked but it was too late. There were several witnesses. I was only doing about thirty. I wasn't charged or anything. Oh, God, he wouldn't? Not after all this time.'

They had already checked; neither of the Vickers had a record. If he'd even been charged with careless driving they'd have been on to it sooner.

'She wasn't dead. Someone called an ambulance and she was taken to Redlands. I telephoned several times during the night. She died in the operating theatre. The Coroner said it was an accident. I didn't even get an endorsement. It took me a long time to get over it, I didn't use the car for ages.'

'That's right,' Julie said. 'I wasn't with him at the time it happened, but for ages afterwards it was all he could talk about. He had nightmares too.'

'I wrote to her parents afterwards, and went to see them several times. It was as if I couldn't keep away, as if by going to see them it would make it all right. I thought I knew what they were going through. I didn't. I know now all right. Oh Sharon, Sharon, have I done this to you?'

Julie put her arm around him, offering comfort she didn't want to give. There was somewhere to place the blame now. On Tom.

1982, eleven years ago, the Chief calculated. It was a long time to wait for revenge.

'What was the name of the child, Mr Vickers?'

'Elizabeth. Elizabeth Blake.'

Blake. He'd seen him. Others had seen him. He had put him down as no more than a recluse. Why hadn't he listened to local gossip? And if he was the same Blake he would have been over fifty when the child Vickers killed was born. Could it be him?

'Thank you both. I'm sorry if we've added to your distress, but we had to know. Where do the Blakes live now?'

173

Tom and Julie looked at each other. They shook their heads.

'In Rickenham Green the last time I saw them, but that was ten years ago.'

Ian and Barry were about to get into their car when they saw the portly figure of Sergeant Davies hurrying towards them. 'Sir, sir!' he called, panting.

'We were on our way to see you, Sergeant.'

'I think we've got him, sir. Blake. George Blake.'

'Yes,' Ian replied, without showing the slightest surprise, 'I think we have.'

But George Blake was not at home.

In the end they broke into the stone cottage without applying for a search warrant. If Blake was the man they wanted not a minute must be wasted. There might be others he wished to harm, or even kill. If it was over, he might have decided to take his own life and could be inside, already dead or dying. A man obsessional enough to wait eleven years was capable of anything.

They had knocked at the front and back doors, and posted men at each of them in case he tried to make a run for it. Everything was securely locked. They let themselves in through the back way by breaking a pane of glass and undoing the door with the key in the lock inside. There was no corpse, neither was there any sign of life. Everything appeared much as it had when Sergeant Davies last called. The place had not been cleaned up, papers and dishes were left wherever they'd last been used and there was a bowl on the floor containing scraps of dog food which were fresh. Blake had not been gone more than a few hours at the most and had taken the dog with him.

'I don't think I've ever seen him without Beth,' Sergeant Davies commented. 'Takes her everywhere.' That should make finding him a little easier; a man with a dog was more noticeable.

They searched the house but found nothing of interest downstairs.

'Holy Moses!' Sergeant Davies said when he opened the door of what was obviously the room in which Blake slept. 'Take a look at this.'

In a corner was a table. On it was a large, unadorned crucifix and it was surrounded with photographs of a child showing her progress from babyhood until the time she died. She was not a pretty child and her mouth showed signs of petulance, but Blake had obviously adored her. Underneath the table were some of her toys and exercise books, containing schoolwork. A lock of her hair was fixed on to a sheet of plain, white card and placed carefully behind the glass of a photo frame. There was no question, Blake was obsessive. The Chief felt these things should have been put away many years ago, to be brought out and looked at now and again as a happy reminder of a loved child, not left in view to fuel whatever feelings the man was harbouring. He moved closer. There was a sheet of paper under the picture frame. On it was a list of names. The first four had a red line drawn through them. They knew three of those names, but not the fourth – Sandra Cooper. The fifth, William Harding, had to be the next victim. The Chief showed it to Bob Davies.

'Not local, sir. No one in the village by that name.'

'Get on to Redlands immediately,' he told Barry Swan. 'See if he's known there.' Barry went downstairs to make the call. He was informed by the lady in Records that there used to be a William Harding, a surgeon, but he retired three or four years ago. She went off to find his address. Barry recognized the area – it was eminently suitable for a surgeon who had done well for himself. Maple Drive was on the outskirts of the town, tree-lined, with large, detached houses either side. He picked up Blake's out-of-date telephone directory and looked for the number. It was not listed. Of course, he would be ex-directory. He rang headquarters and asked them to get someone on to it right away. Harding had to be warned. A message came back via the car radio that a family named Johnson lived there now. The Hardings had moved three years ago; they were trying to locate them.

'What now?' the Chief asked. 'What if Blake knows where he

is? We might be too late.' They had come to the correct conclusion that Harding was the man who performed the unsuccessful operation on Elizabeth. His fate also had to be death.

10

They had traced William Harding. They had, in fact, found quite a lot of them but a quick visit to the house where he used to live confirmed that the one they were looking for had moved to Frampton. The Johnsons did not know the address but remembered him saying that's where they were going.

'Local, after all,' the Chief said after they had given instructions to the Frampton police. 'I just hope we're not too late.'

Barry Swan hoped it was going to be one of those situations in which the CID rushed in to save the victim at the last minute. It would look good on his record. But there had been no answer to their telephone call, so more than likely they were out. Besides, the Frampton police would be there ahead of them and an APB had been transmitted giving Blake's registration number.

Two miles outside Frampton the radio crackled into life.

'Sandra Cooper, sir,' the disembodied voice told them, 'died six years ago.' They held their breath. Had Blake been steadily killing people since the death of his own child? 'Killed when a light aircraft she was travelling in came down in the mountains. She was on her way to join a mission in Africa.'

They sighed in unison.

'For a minute there I thought . . .' Barry said.

'So did I,' the Chief replied.

Ahead of them they saw several parked cars, two of them patrol cars. In the back of one, making no attempt to move, was George Blake.

'DCI Roper,' Ian said to the man who approached him. 'Is that Blake?'

'Yes, sir. No question. He was sitting in his car with the dog when we got here. This was on the front seat.' He handed Ian a plastic bag containing a lethal-looking knife. 'He's not said a word. Gave us his name with no trouble, then clammed up.'

'OK, thanks. We'll take it from here. Your men can go now.'

George Blake allowed himself to be led to one of the Rickenham cars, handcuffed to Barry Swan. He said nothing until they pulled up outside the station, and all he said then was, 'I knew I should have done it yesterday.'

On Wednesday evening while she waited for the vegetables to boil, Janet Penhaligon listened to the radio. The boys preferred television and were watching it in the other room. Jacko had no interest in either and was still not back from work. She was not aware when the music stopped and the news began until she heard the name Sharon Vickers. Her mouth went dry. And then, while the potatoes, left to their own devices, boiled over, she sat at the kitchen table and sobbed as if her heart was breaking. That was how Jacko found her a few minutes later. He looked from the cooker to her, turned off the heat under the ruined food and put his arms around her.

'Janet, love, what is it? The boys?' No more, please God, he couldn't take any more.

'Sharon,' Janet hiccupped, 'Sharon Vickers. They've arrested someone.'

The strength left Jacko's legs. He sank into the kitchen chair beside her. 'Perhaps they'll leave us alone now,' he said as tears of relief ran down his own face.

Michael and Brian, hearing their father's voice, came into the kitchen and looked at each other in mute surprise. Their mother and father sat side by side, an arm around each other, crying. When they saw the boys they began to smile, and then to laugh, until Michael and Brian too, joined in although they hadn't got a clue what they were laughing at. It was a moment of pure happiness.

But grown-ups were strange creatures, laughing and crying at the same time, and worse, there was no sign of tea.

'Fish fingers, now, I'm afraid,' Janet said when they had pulled themselves together.

'Great!' Michael said. 'With beans and chips?'

'And Instant Whip for pudding?' Brian wanted to know. He would eat it every day if Janet did not insist on allowing instant puddings only as a treat.

'Yes,' she said, 'and Instant Whip. Go on, you can make it, but leave some for the rest of us.'

The atmosphere was almost festive in the Penhaligon household that evening. Only when they were in bed did Jacko voice his concern. 'Do you think I should tell them now? What I told you on Friday?'

'No, Jacko, it's too late, but they might still be able to make something of it, you not saying anything. And it doesn't matter now. I know why you did it – it was partly my fault. If I hadn't gone on about the girl so much you probably would've said something. But all you saw was her body, not who killed her.'

'I thought you'd think I did it.'

'I know. But your telling them wouldn't have helped them catch him any quicker.'

'Can we start again? From tomorrow? Try to be happy like we used to be?'

'Mm. We'll try.' Janet was almost asleep, more relaxed than she had been for a very long time.

'George Blake. I can't believe it,' Dorothy said, astounded when her husband gave her the news. 'And to think – oh, Bob, the meat, when Mrs Black saw him in the butcher's in Rickenham, he must've used it to poison the dog. It wasn't for himself after all. And poor Julie and Tom, he's bound to feel it's his own fault. I wonder what they'll do?'

'Sell up, I expect, eventually. I don't suppose they'll want reminders around them all the time. I wish I'd listened a bit more closely when you said about Blake. It is a fact he lives off tinned food, not just gossip. There's enough of it at his place to feed an army.'

'What's going to happen to the dog?'

'Oh, no, you don't. We're not going to have her here. She'll be put down if the RSPCA can't find a home for her. There's another thing, too. Young WPC Robbins asked me how long Blake had lived here, not that she suspected, mind, more out of curiosity, and I meant to ask you. If I had, it might have got me thinking about his daughter. Not that I knew any details, only that she was killed in an accident. I shan't be sorry to retire, you know, I'm beginning to feel I'm not quite quick enough any more.'

'You're quite quick enough for me, Bob Davies. Now, move yourself, I want to get washed up.'

George Blake sat in the interview room staring at the wall. It was over. He had almost succeeded. Very clever of them to have worked it out.

'Don't keep repeating the same questions, please,' he said when his interrogators wanted to start at the beginning again. 'I've told you everything. I'm quite prepared to make a statement. I killed Sharon Vickers. I burned down Margaret Price's house and I killed Adamson's dog. I would've killed Harding if he'd been at home. What more do you want me to say?'

The Hardings had not been in danger, at least not that day. Since his retirement and his wife's subsequent confinement to a wheelchair, they had spent a lot of their time away. William Harding knew what his wife did not. She had not long to live and he wanted to make the few remaining years as happy as possible. They hunted out hotels with the necessary facilities and spent their time in them, enjoying the luxury of being waited on. He was never told of what might have been his fate. There was no point.

'That man was like a time bomb waiting to go off, all that hatred boiling away inside him,' the Chief said when Blake was returned to his cell. 'It's a wonder he didn't crack up long ago. Still, at least there's no doubt. Everything he's told us fits, no one innocent could have given all those details. But imagine, watching and waiting all that time. And to take out his grief on an innocent child. The man's sick.'

'Those last two years must have been pure misery for his wife,' Brian Lord, the police psychologist said. 'She'd already tragically lost her only child and then to have her husband so obsessed he didn't even notice her own condition deteriorating must have been heart-breaking. From what he said, he hardly noiced when she died.' Blake had been aware that his wife had suffered a massive coronary thrombosis and had died at about the same age as her own mother. He preferred to let it be known that she died of a broken heart so that he could blame that, too, on Vickers.

'I still find it hard to believe,' Barry said, as they talked through the case to get it out of their systems, 'that he actually planned the whole thing years ago. What? Ten, eleven years ago? To keep tracks on all those people, spying outside the hospital and getting acquainted with Margaret Price's friends so he knew her routine off by heart, watching Jim Adamson and the Hardings – and the cool nerve, to get theirs and the Vickers' new addresses from next-door neighbours by posing as a relative.'

'He was a very sick man,' Brian Lord continued. 'It happens sometimes. You have to remember that he and his wife were a self-sufficient couple, quite disturbed when they found she was pregnant at her age, but then the baby, Elizabeth, changed their lives. They lived for her. As Blake said, she gave him something to look forward to in old age. What he did to his victims was what he thought they had done to him. He took away what mattered most. Tom Vickers, that was obvious. Margaret Price has no relatives, nothing she cared more about than the house she had saved so hard for. It'll never seem the same to her. Adamson, well, he's divorced, his wife and family are in

Glasgow; Blake couldn't get at him through them, there were too many bad feelings for Adamson to care, but King, the dog, that was a different matter.'

'I don't know what to think,' Ian said. 'First he was going to kill Ronnie once he was eight, but when he discovered Mrs Vickers was pregnant again he waited to see if it was a girl. How would they feel if they knew? I've only got the one son, but if I had more and knew it could have been the other child, would I resent the existence of the one who lived?'

'You can't think about it,' Brian told him. 'You mustn't. It'll drive you crazy. And hopefully they'll never know. You can keep that from the press, can't you?' Ian nodded. 'Good. Look, the man was obsessional, his desire for revenge was eating away at him. He lived every minute with only one thought in his mind. Probably he wasn't very stable to start with. It isn't usual to believe a Casualty sister, a nurse and a hospital porter are deliberately trying to avoid saving your child's life, that the reason Adamson and the girl that was killed in the plane crash, the nurse – what was her name?'

'Cooper,' Ian said. 'Sandra Cooper.'

'Yes, that they pushed that trolley slowly for any other reason than the one they gave him, that any sudden movement would endanger her further. She was, after all, going to have brain surgery.'

'Will an insanity plea hold water?' Ian wanted to know.

'Maybe not any more. Part of it was the waiting. It was the only thing that kept him going. Did he sound insane to you? He's got nothing left now, those years of wanting revenge kept him going. My own feelings are that whatever the courts do to him, it won't be enough. He'll fade quietly away, he's lost the will to live. You heard what he said, no one wishes the death penalty was still in existence more than Blake.'

'I wonder if he's any idea what it's like inside for child murderers?' Barry said.

They talked it out, the three of them, until there was nothing more left to say.

'Home, I think,' Ian said. 'You, too, Barry. We'll leave the rest until the morning.'

'Yes, sir.' Barry was glad, very glad this awful day was over; it had taken its toll on all of them. There was lots to think about, many things about human nature that were new to him. He looked at his watch. There was plenty of time to shower and change before he went to collect Lucy. At least he wouldn't have to keep her waiting. He could begin to look forward to it. He said goodnight and left.

'Never crossed my mind it was a dog Mrs Morris saw him carrying. Sergeant Davies said he never goes anywhere without it. He even took it with him when he went to kill Sharon.'

'He admitted the dog was his excuse for being in the woods,' Brian said. 'He only got it once he realized Sharon spent a lot of time up there. It would have looked odd if he was alone.'

'And it hadn't crossed *his* mind that Beth wouldn't leave the body alone once he'd done it. It must've taken some doing, a man of that age, in a hurry, carrying a collie on a hot day.'

'OK, Ian. Enough for tonight. Go home and think about anything at all, anything except George Blake.'

Ian left the station and went out to where his car was parked. He waved to Barry who was bending down speaking to Judy Robbins through the open window of her own car.

'You must feel pleased with yourselves,' she was saying.

'Yes, we do. Thank God it's over. Sorry, I can't stop though, I'm on my way to meet Lucy.'

Judy looked him full in the face. He wasn't joking. 'Well,' she said, grinning back, 'all I can say is, good luck.'

If a level-headed, warm, intelligent girl like Lucy wanted a second night out with the infamous Sergeant Swan, he must have something good going for him.

Helen Campbell wanted to go home. She was not a nutter like the people around her, and she was frightened. She had never set foot in a psychiatric hospital before, although this was only a ward at Redlands. Deceiving Alan with those awful videos was wrong, she knew that, but she had to admit she got some sort of a kick out of it. And the money was good. She was a fake through and through. Even the suicide attempt was not genuine. She had known perfectly well that what she was taking could not kill her – she did it because she was manipulative, she knew what it would do to Alan and that he would forgive her. She did not think she had a problem; she did not realize that her doctor saw through her manipulations, which in themselves were a cause for concern. Well-balanced people do not attempt suicide even knowing it will be unsuccessful. In the two discussions that had already taken place between them, the doctor had seen the extent of Helen Campbell's inferiority complex and it puzzled him anew that patients who outwardly had everything going for them often displayed her symptoms while other, less attractive people, those with no talent and sometimes no job or family to boost their confidence, coped perfectly well. With her husband's support Mrs Campbell would – what? Not recover, she wasn't really ill. Mature. That was the word. She gave the impression that she thought of herself more as Mr Campbell's child than his wife. He arranged to see her once a month.

'Ian, you're early again. What's going on?' Moira asked as she put her shopping bags down in the hallway, having only returned herself at that moment. 'If I'd known, you could have given me a lift with this lot.'

But then she saw the strain in his face, the lines of utter fatigue etched there. She also saw that he was starting to relax. His body was not held rigid. No matter how many hours he put in, no matter how much sleep he missed while a case was in progress, the effects only really showed when it was over. Ian rubbed his forehead with the tips of his fingers and told her as much.

'It's over,' he said. 'We've got him. And I'm sick of it all, I'm jacking it in.'

'The job?' Moira was flabbergasted. Not once in all their years together had there been a single moment when she thought she would hear him say such a thing.

'You need a drink, and a bath, and then another drink,' she said. 'Then you can tell me all about it.'

Ian nodded and obeyed her instructions as if he was a small child. Moira went to run the bath. As hot as the weather was, she filled it with steaming water until the tank was empty before adding some cold. 'Get in,' she commanded. 'I'll bring you a whisky.'

He was exhausted and disgusted with life and lay in the bath hoping some of the filth of what he had to deal with would be washed away.

Moira left him for half an hour then took his dressing-gown in to him. 'Here, don't bother to get dressed again, you won't be going out.'

'Thanks, love.' Some of the vileness had been washed away, but not all of it – not all the misery, nor the contamination of human behaviour. And there was still Ross.

He dried himself, feeling bodily, if not mentally, refreshed, and went downstairs carrying his empty glass. He sat in his comfortable armchair and Moira poured him another drink and a gin and tonic for herself.

'Do you want to talk about it?'

'I don't think I'm cut out for it any more. It seems to be getting to me and I used to be able to stand back and be objective. Kids getting killed, it's too much.' Ian's lips tightened. 'Oh, it's not just that, it's everything. Campbell and his wife, and those videos – if you could have seen what was in some of them, it's enough to make most people vomit. They're animals, people who do that, nothing but bloody animals. And Tom Vickers, he's going to blame himself for both of those children's deaths now until the day he dies, and perhaps his wife won't be able to live with it either.'

Moira didn't know what he was talking about, she thought only one child had been killed. Ian explained but she was hardly listening; the thought of him not being a policeman had shaken her. There had been many times when she'd wished he had a nice, safe office job, but now he'd said the words, she knew she didn't wish that at all. Ian was meant to be a policeman; he had the right values and attitudes. He couldn't, mustn't give it up.

Ian's glass was empty. He got up for a refill, pouring a measure even more generous than his wife's had been. Moira held out her own glass. If it was going to be one of those nights, she might as well join him.

'Ross,' he said. 'I've got that little matter to deal with tomorrow. The Chief Constable has requested my presence.' This was said with more than a touch of sarcasm, not Ian's usual style, and suddenly Moira saw it all. Ian did not want to leave the force, bad as the last few days had been – he was mentally preparing himself for tomorrow, for the time when he might be asked to leave. She was not sure what was going on between him and Ross, only that it wasn't good. She knew Ian better than she knew any other human being. Quitting was one thing; being asked for his resignation would be the end of the man as he was now. She questioned her own ability to live with a different Ian Roper.

'Can you tell me, about Ross?'

'There's an inquiry. He's suspended on full pay until it's over.'

'An inquiry?'

'He was trying to haul me off a case before we were finished. I thought he knew something. It's to do with his brother, I can't say more than that. I tried endless times to contact him and ask him to his face, but he's been avoiding me. I had to go over his head. If I'm wrong . . .' But he didn't want to voice what could happen if he was.

'If you're right?'

'His rank's against him. The public won't be satisfied with early retirement or a resignation. A bent PC gets a few lines in the paper, a superintendent will make headlines.'

'And he'll lose his pension.'

Ian nodded.

186

'Poor man.' Moira felt a second's pity. All those years of building a career down the drain. The higher you climb . . .

'I think he thinks he's invincible. And I did disobey his orders. It's not the done thing to go against the big boys.'

'Do you want something to eat?' Ian's glass was nearly empty again. She felt he needed something to soak up the drink.

'No, not at the moment. You have something.'

'Not until you do. Later, then. Mark's out for the night, he's over at Danny's, so we don't have to worry about him. They're bringing him home at ten thirty.'

By the time Mark returned Ian was in bed. 'In bed?' he said when Moira asked him not to make any noise. 'At this time of night?' Mark's eye fell on the whisky decanter on the tray on the sideboard. 'Drunk, I suppose,' he said with the disparaging tone the young have for their elders when they do not behave like their betters.

'He's very tired. The case is solved,' Moira answered, giving nothing away. Mark merely looked at the glass in her own hand, his expression conveying his opinion that his parents were becoming alcoholic.

'You made it on time,' Lucy said with some surprise when she answered the door bell at precisely eight o'clock. 'Come in. It's not much, but, as they say, it's home.'

She shared a flat with two girls and a man, explaining that they were lucky – Terry was the tidiest of the four of them. Barry was not sure he liked the idea of Lucy living in the same house as the handsome creature who was sprawled out on the settee watching television.

She introduced the two men. Terry unfolded himself to his full six feet three inches and held out his hand. Barry took it, groaning inwardly. There were far too many tall men on the planet.

Barry found himself opening the car door for her. 'Easy, sunshine,' he told himself. 'Don't forget there're plenty more out there.'

They had a couple of drinks then went for an Italian meal. The evening passed quickly; they found they had lots to talk about. One thing was certain, though, they couldn't go back to her place, not with Terry bloody Mitchell next door listening to the bedsprings squeaking.

As he drove away from her flat he could not believe it. He had delivered her home, before midnight, without giving her more than a paternal kiss on the cheek. He was seeing her again on Saturday night.

Ian fell into a deep sleep at once, but it didn't last long. He woke a little after three and remained awake for the rest of the night. Not wishing to disturb Moira he crept downstairs and, without bothering to shave or make a drink, drove into work. He remedied both omissions once he was there. He sat at his desk and tied up the loose ends of the Vickers case then gave up any other paperwork as a bad job.

The morning dragged but at last the appointed time came when he could reasonably set off for his meeting with the Chief Constable and the other top brass without arriving far too early.

'Come in, Chief Inspector. Have a seat.'

Ian did so, feeling, he suspected, much as many people must have done when he had used those words.

'We have already spoken to several other people concerned in this matter but we would like to hear what you have to say and your reasons for disobeying orders.'

So this was it then. He had been wrong, misjudged the man and gone out on a limb without consulting anyone. The best he could hope for was demotion.

'Sir, I'm not strictly certain I disobeyed orders. We already had Lloyd in custody and Morgan may have been a suspect in another inquiry. I did what I believed was best. And Lloyd gave me information which I felt could not be ignored.'

'And this information might, or might not, have concerned Superintendent Ross.'

'Yes, sir.'

'Why didn't you put it to Ross before coming to me?'

'I tried, sir, as I said when I spoke to you, on more than one occasion. He ignored my calls. I couldn't leave it as it was. If Superintendent Ross had wanted to, he could have ignored me for ever.'

'I see.'

'Perhaps I've been very stupid, but it only added to my suspicions. I felt that if he knew nothing about his brother's involvement there was no reason why we couldn't continue.' Ian was shaking from head to foot, but at least he had had the chance to say what he'd come to say.

'Thank you for your time, Chief Inspector, that'll be all. We'll be in touch.'

Ian hesitated, unable to believe he was being dismissed in this manner, as if he was of no account. How bloody unfair. And how typical. The least they could do was give him the bad news now. Or didn't they have the guts? Would it come in the form of a memo?

He drove back to Rickenham in a foul mood. He hated things hanging over him.

He stomped upstairs, not even bothering to acknowledge the officer on the desk who greeted him. He slammed his office door behind him as hard as he could.

He was fuming. It was a cover-up, he should have guessed. Ross knew too many important people. He got through the day somehow, feeling calmer by the time he went home. He had the grace to apologize to a secretary whom he had called an incompetent idiot. He looked at his name and rank on the piece of plastic affixed to his door and wondered how much longer it would remain there.

On Friday afternoon Barry received a call from Lucy. He took it in a room where he could speak in privacy.

'I'm so excited,' she told him. 'I'm going on a course. It's for promotion. I applied for it a few months ago, but someone's dropped out and I've got their place this time.'

'That's great. Well done.' So Lucy was as smart as she was pretty. 'When does it start?'

'Monday. I can't believe it, it's such short notice.'

'Monday. Does that mean you're not free tomorrow?'

'Oh, no, but I'm so pleased, I just couldn't wait to tell you. I'm sorry – perhaps I shouldn't have rung you at work.'

'No problem.' He was flattered. 'Where is it, the course?'

'London.'

'London?'

'Yes, you know, the capital of England?'

Barry knew all right. London, with someone as gorgeous as Lucy and a hotel room at her disposal.

'Where are you staying?' He was really rubbing salt in the wound now.

'Oh, a small hotel near Paddington. There're ten of us altogether. It should be great fun. I've only been to London for the odd day, never as long as this.'

'How long is as long as this?'

'A month.'

So this was it, the big kiss-off. Why couldn't she do the damn course in Ipswich?

'But I'll be coming home at weekends,' she was saying. 'Or, if you like, you could come down one weekend and we could do the sights or something.'

'Yes.' Barry coughed. That 'yes' had been a little too high-pitched. 'Yes, that would be lovely. I'll see you tomorrow then.'

He replaced the receiver; several colleagues raised their eyebrows questioningly and grinned when they heard the oh so cool, oh so irresistible Sergeant Swan give a whoop of pleasure from behind the closed door.

Ian slept no better on Thursday night and by the time he got to work on Friday had decided to clear his desk and leave it as tidy as possible for his replacement. Moira was of the opinion that if they intended doing anything about Ian's position, they would have said so at the time, but he was convinced the powers that be were against him.

'For God's sake, Ian!' she said that morning as she slapped a plate of buttered toast in front of him. 'You're beginning to sound paranoid!'

It was getting on towards lunchtime but for once Ian did not think he would be able to eat. He continued sorting out his tray. There were memos and circulars long out of date. He binned them.

'Come in,' he grunted, in response to a knock at his door. As soon as he saw who it was he stood up.

'Good afternoon. Sorry to disturb you,' the Chief Constable said. 'I thought, under the circumstances, I ought to introduce Michael Thorne to you personally.'

Credit where credit's due, Ian decided – he's come himself to introduce my successor.

'Michael's transferring here from Birmingham, and as from next Monday, will be replacing Superintendent Ross. Michael, this is Detective Chief Inspector Ian Roper.'

Ian held out his hand and heartily shook the one offered. 'I am *very* pleased to meet you,' he said, smiling broadly.

Superintendent Thorne could not have known just how pleased.